"YOU DID IT!" SHE CRIED. "OH, DANIEL, YOU DID IT!"

"Of course I did," he responded, his arms closing around her waist and lifting her off the floor. "Did you think I could not with such a taskmaster driving me?"

"Taskmaster? How dare you call me that, you wretch! Put me down this moment!"

"And if I don't?" he taunted, lifting her higher so she was gazing down into his eyes. "What will you do then, my sweet tyrant?"

Penelope started to answer, but the sight of his mouth, inches from her own, drove the words from her mind. Her hands clenched on his muscular shoulders. She could feel his muscles tense, and then he was slowly lowering her until she could feel the warmth of his breath feathering her lips.

And then his mouth was covering hers in a kiss that drove any thoughts of protest from her mind.

The Learned Lady

JOAN OVERFIELD

AVON BOOKS NEW YORK

THE LEARNED LADY is an original publication of Avon Books. This work has never before appeared in book form. This work is a novel. Any similarity to actual persons or events is purely coincidental.

AVON BOOKS
A division of
The Hearst Corporation
1350 Avenue of the Americas
New York, New York 10019

Copyright © 1996 by Joan Overfield
Published by arrangement with the author
Library of Congress Catalog Card Number: 95-94628
ISBN: 0-380-78005-4

First Avon Books Printing: January 1996

AVON TRADEMARK REG. U.S. PAT. OFF. AND IN OTHER COUNTRIES, MARCA REGISTRADA, HECHO EN U.S.A.

Printed in the U.S.A.

RA 10 9 8 7 6 5 4 3 2 1

To Natasha Kern, super-agent extraordinaire!
My thanks for everything.

Author's Note

Many of the experiments mentioned in this book were actually performed by Michael Faraday, a colleague of Sir Humphrey Davy, mentioned here. As Mr. Faraday was a gentleman, I am sure he would not mind letting a lady lay temporary claim to his work.

I should also like to add a special word of thanks to Patricia Phillips for her wonderful book *The Scientific Lady: A Social History of Woman's Scientific Interests 1520–1918*. It proved invaluable in my research.

1

Bibury, England
1815

If the study of science had taught Miss Penelope Grantham anything, it was that not all experiments met with success. No matter how careful one tried to be, things occasionally went awry. When they did, one didn't flee the laboratory in hysterics (unless flames or dangerous chemicals were involved), one stayed and observed the resulting catastrophe. Therefore, when the letter from The Royal Society of Scientific Inquiry arrived in the morning's post, Penelope didn't panic. She read the tersely worded missive, reviewed the facts as she knew them, and then arrived at what seemed to her the only logical conclusion.

"Blast it to flinters, I need a man!"

"And about time too, I should think," Phillipa Grantham responded, not glancing up from the tapestry she was repairing. "Independence in a female is well and good, but I see no reason why you should end your days a spinster. Whom shall you marry?"

It took Penelope a few moments to make sense of her mama's reply, and when she did she gave an impatient shake of her head. "No, mama, I am not talking about marrying a man, I am talking about borrowing one."

1

"Borrowing one?" Mrs. Grantham set her needle aside and frowned. "Don't be daft, child. Ladies do not go about borrowing men. It sounds most hideously improper, and I am quite sure your papa would never have approved."

Considering this entire contretemps was all her father's idea, Penelope was not so certain of that. "Papa was a scientist," she reminded her mother, rising from her chair to pace the parlor. "He would have approved of whatever was the most logical solution to the situation."

"Yes, but what is the situation?" her mother asked, her expression chiding as she studied Penelope. "You really haven't said, you know."

Penelope hesitated a moment before replying. "The Royal Society wishes Ulysses to present his latest experiment at their next public lecture," she said, wishing there was some way she could gentle the blow.

Mrs. Grantham's hazel eyes grew wide with astonishment. "Is that all?" she asked with a laugh, resuming her work on the tapestry. "From that Friday face you are wearing, I thought the matter a serious one. Just put them off with your usual tale of his delicate condition, and all will be well."

"I tried that," Penelope answered grimly, removing the letter from the pocket of her apron and handing it to her mother. "They write if he does not appear they will have no choice but to revoke his grant and award it to another scientist."

"*What?*" Mrs. Grantham exclaimed, scanning the letter anxiously. "Oh no! They can't do this to you . . . can they?"

"I greatly fear they can," Penelope replied, rubbing her aching head with a weary hand. "One of the conditions of accepting the grant was that Ulysses make himself available should the committee desire his presence. I've been able to put them off for the past three years, but now they are insisting."

"My poor darling!" Mrs. Grantham rose from behind her frame and hurried over to embrace Penelope. "There, there," she crooned, giving Penelope's back a maternal pat. "I know you must be disappointed, but it will all turn out right in the end." She drew back and regarded Penelope thoughtfully.

"I do not suppose *you* could go there in Ulysses's stead?"

she suggested. "As far as they know you have been serving as his assistant, and are familiar with his work."

"I've already suggested that," Penelope said with a dispirited sigh. "Their response was to inform me that ladies are not permitted to address the membership. Even if they do make up a significant portion of that membership," she added, unable to keep the bitterness from creeping into her voice.

"Yes, I saw that," Mrs. Grantham said, looking crestfallen. "Oh dear, how very awkward, to be sure."

Despite the bleakness of the situation, Penelope couldn't help but smile at her mama's gift of understatement. Awkward, she decided with a flash of gallows humor, was a very mild word to describe what the Royal Society was likely to view as a case of deliberate deceit, if not outright fraud. Indeed, were they ever to discover the Mr. Ulysses Grantham they had been funding all these years was in fact a female, Penelope would consider herself fortunate not to be clapped in Bridewell!

The idea for her to pose as her brother had started out as something of a family joke. After her last request for patronage had been rejected, her papa had teasingly remarked that she might have fared better had she usurped her brother's name. It wasn't as if Ulysses would either notice or even care, he had added with one of his impish grins, and a scientific society was certain to view a letter from a Mr. Ulysses Grantham with a far kinder eye than they had hers.

At first Penelope had laughed in response, but the more she thought of it, the more sense it made. She knew her hypothesis involving the nature of electricity was sound, but without the backing of an important organization like the Royal Society, there was no way she could prove it. Oh, ladies journals would doubtlessly publish her articles as they had in the past, but without the approval of the greater scientific community, her theories had no hope of ever gaining wide acceptance. That was when her decision to impersonate Ulysses had been born.

Knowing she could never hope to maintain a public pose as a man, she'd coolly decided to make use of Ulysses's pretensions of being an invalid, making him an eccentric who shunned others because of his uncertain health. The deception had worked better than she could have hoped, and in less than three months Ulysses had been granted a considerable stipend by the same society who had rejected her proposal. The irony of that had delighted her papa, who said he considered it the best form of revenge she could have hoped for.

"Well, I suppose it was bound to end sometime or another." Her mother had returned to the settee, and was picking up her needle again. "I am certain you shall miss corresponding with the other scientists and having your work published so quickly, but I have no doubt you shall scrape by somehow."

"I have no intention of scraping by," Penelope protested, resuming her pacing. "I am but a few months from proving that electricity is composed of both positive and negative matter, and I see no reason why I should abandon my research now. There must be something I can do."

"I do not see what," Mrs. Grantham said, repairing another rend in the tapestry. "The Society has made their decision quite plain, and I do not think even you can bully them into changing their minds. Mankind has managed to rattle along quite nicely without your understanding of electricity, and I am sure it will do quite well for another few years at least. Let it go, dearest; it's for the best."

Penelope managed to bite back an angry retort, knowing her mother didn't mean to be hurtful. She had never understood her passionate devotion to science, and seemed to regard it as some freakish flaw in her nature that her daughter would eventually outgrow.

"Why don't you speak to Ulysses?" Her mother asked, shooting her a hopeful look. "Perhaps if you convince him this is some sort of quest he'll agree to play along. You know he fancies himself a sort of knight-errant; there should be nothing he'd enjoy better than a chance to rescue a lady in distress."

"Not if it entails journeying to London," Penelope responded, having already considered and rejected this solution. "He seldom leaves his rooms these days except to stroll by the river or roam about the keep in that old suit of armor of his."

"That is so," her mother agreed, her shoulders drooping in defeat. "Was ever a poor mother so bedeviled? A daughter who tinkers with nature, and a son who thinks he is Don Quixote. And where did he get the idea he is consumptive, I should like to know? Until the fever carried off your papa, no member of this family ever succumbed to anything so common as a *disease*."

The mention of her father brought a small pang to Penelope's heart. It had been almost two years since he had died from a virulent fever, and she missed him still. If only he were here, he would know what to do, she thought sadly. The idea made her pause, and she turned toward the door.

Her mother glanced up from her work. "Where are you going?"

"To see Papa," Penelope said, bending to brush a kiss over her mother's cheek. "Don't worry; I'll be back in time for tea."

"Papa?" Her mother was beginning to look decidedly alarmed. "Why are you going there?"

Penelope hesitated, her hand on the door's handle. "Because," she said, "I've decided this entire fiasco is all his doing. Posing as Ulysses was his idea; let him be the one to get us out of it." With that she turned and left the parlor, her shoulders set with determination.

IN MEMORY OF DANIEL AUGUSTUS WARFIELD
THIRD SON OF RICHARD ALLEN WARFIELD,
VISCOUNT BURLINGTON, OF THIS VILLAGE
DIED AT SEA 18 APRIL 1799
AGE 20 YRS 4 MOS 5 DAYS

Daniel Warfield stood before the plain monument, his face betraying not so much as a flicker of emotion as he studied the epitaph carved into the stone's smooth surface. So the old tyrant had really done it, he thought, a bitter smile twisting his mouth. His father had warned him that if he persisted in pursuing his own desires rather than following family tradition he would consider him dead. It seemed he had kept his word.

He studied his own memorial for several more moments before moving on to the graves of his parents and his elder brothers. His throat grew painfully tight as he studied the dates chiseled into the pristine marble. All dead within five years of each other, he realized, his green eyes growing bleak with loss.

Even though he'd had the long weeks during the voyage from Charleston to accustom himself to the deaths of his parents and brothers, seeing their graves overwhelmed him with grief and horror. What the devil happened? he anguished, laying a trembling hand on Richard's tombstone. Richard had been but thirty-eight when he had died, and James three years younger than that, and less than twelve months separated their deaths. How could two such young men die so quickly and so close to one another?

He lingered in the graveyard another quarter hour, noting with sadness the graves or memorials of several friends. He knew the wars with Napoleon were responsible for most of them, and he felt a familiar stab of guilt that he had passed the wars tucked safely away in America while his schoolmates bled and died fighting Napoleon's brutal tyranny.

Was that how James had died? he wondered, returning to stand before his brother's grave. Daniel had become an American citizen shortly after emigrating to Charleston, and when war had broken out between the two countries he'd given brief thought to joining the American Army. But in the end he hadn't been able to stomach the thought of killing fellow Englishmen, and so he'd done his best to maintain a cautious neutrality. Now he wondered if James had been one of the hundreds of British soldiers who had fallen in the bloody Battle of New Orleans. The thought brought a sheen of unshed tears to his eyes.

He was wrestling with a confusing tangle of emotions when he heard the sound of the rusty iron gate swinging open. He turned his head just as a young woman wrapped in a plaid cloak entered the graveyard, her arms filled with flowers. Realizing she hadn't seen him, he stepped behind one of the larger tombstones, hoping to hide himself. He'd just arrived in the neighborhood, and was in no mood to explain his presence to anyone. Besides, he told himself, watching as she made her way to one of the newer graves, it was obvious the poor woman was in mourning and wouldn't welcome his company.

He continued watching as she paused in front of a grave, the hood of her cloak falling back to reveal an untidy chignon of dark blond curls. She stood there for several seconds before opening her arms, letting the flowers fall to the grave in a colorful rain of blossoms.

"Well, I hope you are satisfied," he heard her say in a waspish tone. "We are all knee-deep in the scandal broth now, and it is all your doing!"

Daniel's lips twitched. Her accents were those of a lady, if the sentiments were not, and he wondered what the occupant of the grave had done to earn her displeasure. He decided to make a discreet departure, and pushed open the wrought-iron gate separating his family's plot from the rest of the churchyard. The gate gave a rusty screech of protest, and the woman leapt to her feet and whirled about to face him.

"Who is there?" she demanded, a scowl on her face as she peered into the shadows cast by the looming headstones. "Whoever you are, come out where I can see you!"

Daniel's smile widened at the querulous demand, and he stepped out into the sunlight streaming through the ancient yew planted beside his family's gravesite.

"My apologies, ma'am," he said, sketching a mocking bow in her direction. "I thought you wished to be private in your grief, and had no wish to intrude. Pray accept my apologies if I frightened you."

Eyes an exotic blend of green and gold flashed at his words. "I wasn't in the least frightened!" She stood her ground defiantly. "It is just I do not care for being spied upon by strange . . . persons." Her gaze swept over him in a manner that was deliberately insulting.

Daniel's eyes narrowed in anger. He was cursed if he'd allow the little termagant to treat him like an encroaching cit when he'd done nothing to warrant it.

"I have already offered an explanation for my actions," he said, his voice icy with pride. "If you find it unsatisfactory, then we have nothing to say to one another. Good day." He turned and began walking away when he heard her call out.

"Sir!"

He swung back around to face her. "Yes?"

A light flush stained her cheeks as she made her way to where he was standing. "I wish to apologize," she said, her voice as stiff as her expression. "I did not mean to be offensive."

He was too angry to grant her any quarter. "Yes, you did."

Her flush deepened at the clipped words. "You are right," she admitted, meeting his gaze. "I did. I was in a foul temper, and I fear I took that temper out upon you. It was very wrong of me, and I would ask that you would forgive me. I am sorry."

Her frankness, as well as the honesty he saw shimmering in her hazel eyes, did much to dispel Daniel's anger, and he relaxed enough to send her a cool smile. "I apologize as well. I should have made my presence known as soon as I saw you."

An answering smile touched her soft lips before she turned in the direction where she'd first seen him. Her eyes widened as she read the names carved in the marble tablets.

"Do you know the Burlingtons, sir?" she asked, sounding faintly curious.

Daniel was uncertain how to reply, realizing the difficult position in which he found himself. Because of his father's duplicity, Daniel Warfield was assumed to be dead, so there was no way he could honestly introduce himself without enduring a dozen questions he would as lief not face. He thought quickly before replying.

"Not really. We are related on my mother's side, and I thought to visit them while I am in England."

She started in surprise. "You aren't English?"

"I am Daniel Canton, from Charleston," he said, knowing his friend and business partner would have no objection to his making free with his name. "My mother often mentioned we have family in this area, and I promised her I would call upon them. It seems I am too late." He nodded at the quartet of graves.

Her expression grew somber. "I am sorry," she said gently.

"You must be disappointed to have come so far for naught."

He managed a negligent shrug. "I expected some of them would have died by now," he said, feeling afresh the sting of loss. He hesitated a moment before adding, "I . . . I thought she mentioned her cousins had a fourth son, Andrew. I do not see a stone for him here. Do you know where I might find him?"

She shook her head in regret. "My family and I have lived in the area but a few years, and I fear I have never had the honor of meeting the viscount. I believe he lives in London, however, if that is any help to you."

"Yes, that is a great help, thank you," he answered, understanding why she didn't seem to recognize him. Granted he'd been out of the country for the past fifteen years, but he also bore a strong resemblance to his father, and he'd been waiting for someone to remark on it. Under normal circumstances it would have posed no problem, but now the resemblance presented him with a decided difficulty. Unless he wished to pass himself off as his father's by-blow, he thought cynically, his mouth twisting at the thought of his priggish father unbending enough to take a mistress.

"Are you staying in the neighborhood, Mr. Canton, or will you be journeying to London?" The woman had knelt and was arranging the flowers on the grave.

Again Daniel hesitated, uncertain how to answer. He'd originally planned pausing in Bibury only long enough to visit his family's graves, but being faced with the stark reality of their deaths had affected him more than he'd anticipated. Suddenly the thought of a few days' respite was sweetly tempting, and he reached an abrupt decision.

"I believe I shall be remaining." Then he realized the new set of problems his decision raised. His family's ancestral home lay less than a mile away, but because of the memorial marker his father had erected, there was no way he could appear on the doorstep without inciting a small riot. He'd already arranged for his trunks to be delivered to the townhouse he'd rented in London, but he supposed the few things he had tucked in his valise should be sufficient to see him through the next day or so.

"Perhaps you would be good enough to recommend a hostelry in the area? It needn't be anything grand," he added when she hesitated. "My tastes are simple ones, I assure you."

"I have heard The Blue Jar in the village is adequate," she said, her voice so slow and her manner so thoughtful that Daniel wondered what ailed her. He also recalled the inn from his misspent youth, and wondered if the innkeeper would remember him. Not that there was much chance of that, he decided with a flash of self-deprecation. The man he was now little resembled the pimply-faced youth who'd once sat in the inn's taproom petulantly demanding the finest port.

"The Blue Jar sounds fine," he said, offering her his hand as she rose to her feet. "I thank you for the suggestion, ma'am. I am in your debt."

Instead of answering him right away, the woman stood gazing up at him, her hazel eyes studying his face with a manner which would have been brazen had her expression not been so solemn.

"Mr. Canton, might I ask you something?" she asked at last.

"What is it?" he asked warily, wondering if she had finally noticed his resemblance to the Burlingtons and was about to comment on it.

"Do you have many friends in England?"

He blinked in confusion, wondering if he had heard aright. "I beg your pardon?"

"Do you have many friends? People who might recognize you?"

"Why the devil should you wish to know that?" he demanded, completely baffled.

She gave him a sweet smile. "No reason," she said, her eyes gleaming with some emotion he could not name. "I was merely curious. You say you are American, and yet you sound English."

"And how would you know what an American sounds like? Have you conversed with so many of my countrymen?" he demanded, wondering if he was in the presence of a madwoman.

"No," she admitted, not seeming to be the least bit put off

by his acerbic reply. "But as I said, you sound as proper as a squire saying his vespers, and I was but remarking on it. Were you educated here?"

"Yes," he said, seizing eagerly upon the explanation. "I attended Oxford for half a term before being sent down." Since he was using Geoffrey's name, he might as well make use of his past as well.

"Mmm." She began to tap her foot. "And you're quite certain no one would recognize you? There's no chance some old school chum might come up to you at some inopportune moment, and fall upon you as if you were the prodigal son returned from his travels?"

Her apt analogy made Daniel pale. "How the devil am I to know that?" he demanded harshly, deciding he'd had enough of this odd creature and her equally odd ways. He began backing away, ready to make a dash for it should it prove necessary.

"It's a risk, I suppose," she said, not seeming to notice his furtive movement. "Still, as Papa used to say, no scientific endeavor is without its risks, and at least I shan't have to pry you out of some rusting suit of armor. Yes." She gave a firm nod. "You shall do quite nicely."

Daniel felt a thrill of fear slither down his spine. "Do for what?" he asked, hoping he wouldn't have to use force to subdue her. He'd never raised a hand to a woman, and he disliked the notion of harming one, even in self-defense.

"Why, to pose as my brother, of course," she said, the beatific smile she gave him confirming his worst fears. "But you needn't look so horrified, sir. I am fully prepared to pay you for your pains. Shall we say twenty pounds? Ten now, and ten when the deed is done?"

2

A stunned silence greeted Penelope's offer. "You're mad," Mr. Canton said at last, thrusting a hand through his dark hair and scowling at her. "It's the only possible explanation."

This was a charge Penelope had heard before, and she dismissed it with a wave of her hand. "Nonsense, sir. I have never been in better control of my faculties," she said, her heart racing with excitement. She felt just as she did when an experiment took an unexpected turn, and it was all she could do to restrain herself.

Mr. Canton's expression changed from caution to cynicism. "You will forgive me if I fail to be reassured, madam," he drawled, his green gaze flicking over her in a manner that bordered on insolence. "So far your behavior has done nothing to convince me you are anything other than a moonling."

Penelope's pleasure wavered at his harsh accusation. "I am not a moonling," she said, gritting her teeth to keep her temper in check. "I am a scientist."

He raised a dark eyebrow. "A scientist?"

His hardness made Penelope hesitate. When he'd told her he was an American visiting England, it was as if all her prayers had been answered in one dramatic fell swoop. Who better to impersonate Ulysses than a man no one knew, a man who would be leaving when the charade was done? It had

12

seemed the perfect solution, but now she wasn't so certain. For her plan to succeed she would need his complete cooperation, and she realized that might not be so easily gained. She thought another moment, and then offered him a tentative smile.

"Perhaps we should begin again," she said, deciding the first order of business was to set his mind at ease. "Pray allow me to introduce myself; I am Miss Penelope Grantham. My family and I reside a short distance from here, and I assure you, I am completely respectable."

Mr. Canton stared at her, his austere face revealing none of his thoughts. "Respectable ladies, Miss Grantham, do not go about offering strange gentlemen twenty pounds to pose as their brother," he said in tones of iciest civility. "I might be a visitor here, but even I know such things are not done."

So much for her assuming Americans were more democratic in their notions, she thought, resisting the urge to give his well-shod ankle a swift kick. It appeared they were every bit as priggish as their English brothers.

"I am aware of that," she conceded irritably. "But I have a good reason for what I am asking."

He looked more skeptical than ever. "And what reason might that be? Are you planning to elope against your family's wishes?"

"Of course not!" she denied indignantly. "I am a scientist, and I think far too much of my mind to squander it on some foolish man!"

"Then why do you wish me to pose as your brother?"

Penelope glared up at him in resigned defeat, realizing he wouldn't be satisfied until he'd wrung the entire story from her. She paused for a moment to organize her thoughts, and then proceeded to tell him of her deception and the reasons for it.

"I see," he said, when she'd finished speaking. "You're saying you've been defrauding this Royal Society for the past four years, and they've finally found you out." He gave her a derisive look. "Your forgiveness, Miss Grantham, but it seems to me you're only getting what you deserve. I see no reason why I should help you."

Penelope took instant umbrage to his accusations. "I didn't defraud them!" Her hands clenched in fury. "My experiments and their results were entirely valid!"

"Then the Society should have no problem extending your grant, should they?" he asked, his voice dripping with false sweetness.

For a moment Penelope was strongly tempted to withdraw her offer and tell him to go to the devil, but having come this far, she had no choice but to press ahead. "I have told you," she said, enunciating each word carefully, "they thought the grant was for a *Mr.* Grantham, and if he doesn't appear, I shall be forced to relinquish their patronage. I need their recognition if my experiments are to be taken seriously, and I shall do whatever is necessary to keep it!"

His sneer grew more pronounced. "Greed ill-becomes a scientist, Miss Grantham," he drawled contemptuously. "And again, I see no reason why I should help you."

Penelope's patience shattered at his cutting words. Not even a stipend of fifty pounds per anum was worth enduring such insufferable behavior. "In that case, sir, I shall bid you *adieu*," she said, her voice tight with fury. "I hope you enjoy your stay in our village. Good day." And with that she turned and walked away, her head held high with pride.

After leaving the cemetery, Daniel rode directly to The Blue Jar. Not wishing to draw undue attention, he took the inn's second-best chamber, tipping the innkeeper just enough to insure the bedlinens would be fresh. He also slipped the man's wife a few coins, winning her sullen promise to bring him hot water for his morning's ablutions. He hadn't been dissembling when he'd told Miss Grantham his tastes were simple, but there was a limit to the deprivations he was willing to endure.

Thinking of Miss Grantham made him scowl, and he shook his head in disgust. What an odd creature she was, he thought, staring out the window of his room to the streets below. As pretty as an English rose, with her wavy dark blond hair and sparkling hazel eyes, and a voice as low and sweet as a lark's song. It was a pity her manners weren't nearly as pleasing as her person. A man could be easily tempted by her heart-shaped face, slender, feminine form, and full, tempting lips, but the moment she opened those lips, there was no overlooking the fact she was a shrew of the first water.

And a bluestocking, he added, remembering the deceit she had perpetuated on the Royal Society. He wondered if her hapless brother was aware she had usurped his name and was attempting to hire someone to impersonate him, then decided it was no concern of his. He had other, more pressing matters on his mind at the moment, as well as a host of questions for which he was to determined to find answers.

Once he'd seen to his domestic arrangements he went down to the inn's smoky taproom, hoping to hear some of the local gossip. Clinging to the identity he'd given Miss Grantham, he bought the house several rounds, and while the patrons enjoyed his largesse he began asking careful questions regarding his family.

"Aye, young Richard's death were a hard blow to us all," one man said with a heavy sigh. "Such a shame, it were, comin' as it did less than a year after inheritin' the title from his father. May God bless the old viscount's soul."

"Not that some o' us weren't all that surprised, mark you," a second man opined, taking a deep sip of ale. "The lad were always a neck-or-nothing rider with more bottom than brains."

This blunt description of the elder brother he had secretly worshipped made Daniel wince with pain. Richard had adored horses more than anything, and Daniel recalled hearing him say that he preferred horses to people, as horses were far less self-serving. Richard was one of the finest horsemen he'd ever seen, and he found it troubling that he should die in a riding accident.

"Did anyone ever learn what caused the accident?" he asked, feigning indifference as he signaled for another round. "I remember my mother saying her cousins were all crack riders."

"Oh aye, there never were a Burlington born what couldn't sit a proper saddle," the first man agreed with a nod. "But 'tis just as true there's not a man-jack o'em what can hold their spirits. The young lord was full o' drink and himself, they do say, and took a half-wild stallion out for a midnight

ride. His host tried to stop him, but—'' He gave an expressive
shrug. ''The searchers didn't find him 'til the next mornin',
and by then the poor lad were dead as a post. Broke his fool
neck, he did.''

Daniel's hand closed convulsively about his tankard. Once
in the Carolinas he'd seen one of his friends killed in a fall
from a horse, and Daniel remembered how pitiful he'd looked,
lying in the dust like a broken toy a thoughtless child had cast
away. Then he remembered something else.

It had been about a month before he'd left England, and
he'd ridden to the inn after he and his father had had one of
their infamous rows. He'd taken one of Richard's mounts
without permission, and when he'd returned slightly the worse
for drink, a furious Richard had been waiting for him.

''Only a lackwit would take an animal like this out when
he is jug-bitten,'' he'd raged, giving Daniel a sound shaking.
''I vow, if I hear of you doing such a thing again, I'll box
your ears 'til you howl!''

The shaking, as well as the scold, had stung Daniel's young
pride, but it was the last time he'd ever ridden when he'd been
imbibing. Remembering that, he found it impossible to believe
Richard would have taken a horse, especially an unbroken one,
out for a moonlight ride when he'd been drinking. It went
against everything he remembered of his brother, and he felt
a stir of uneasiness.

''How very sad,'' he drawled, infusing a note of ennui in
his voice and leaning back in his chair. ''Pray where did the
accident happen? Near here?''

'' 'Twere up Yorkshire way,'' another of the patrons vol-
unteered, his filthy face wrinkling in a frown as he struggled
to recall the details. ''Near Hawes, I'm thinkin'.''

''Nay, 'twas nearer to Ripon, you sot!'' the second man
taunted derisively. ''The viscount was stayin' at the Marquess
of Haworth's for a sennight. Don't you remember the takin'
Master James was in when he had to leave his ladybird and
go up to fetch his brother home? Proper furious, he were.''

This sparked a heated debate, and while the others argued
Daniel tried to compose himself. Hearing the details of Ri-

chard's death had stunned him, and he vowed to contact Lord Haworth the moment he reached London.

"And what of this Master James?" he asked when the arguing subsided. "Did he die in a riding accident as well?"

A round of raucous laughter greeted his innocent question. "'Tweren't no ridin' accident," a newcomer gave a scornful snicker. "Only ridin' that young buck ever done was in his bedchamber, if ye'll be takin' my meanin'. 'Twas the pox what carried him off."

"Nay, 'twas the fever!" another man challenged, setting down his tankard with a thump. "My sister was second housemaid at the time, and she said the poor lad sickened and died in less than two days time. No pox ever done *that* to a man!"

"And a blessed thing too, else ye wouldn't be here jawin' at us," the newcomer retorted, much to the amusement of the others.

Daniel ignored their laughter, fearing he would be ill. James had always been robust and hearty, never succumbing to so much as a heavy cold. So how then, he wondered apprehensively, could he have taken ill and died so quickly? As with Richard's death, it made no sense. What the devil had transpired during his long absence? Daniel didn't yet know, but if it was the last thing he did, he was determined to learn the truth.

Penelope spent the next two days vacillating between dark despair and blazing fury. Every time she thought of Mr. Canton's behavior she felt like screeching with disappointment. He was perfect for her needs, and if he'd but considered her offer rationally, he'd have seen the logic of her plans at once. Instead he had flown into a priggish rage, refusing her for no other reason than sheer perversity and arrogant pride.

Pride. An image of Mr. Canton, his dark green eyes simmering with icy rage, flashed in her mind. Perhaps that had been her mistake, she thought, her spirits lifting as she gave the matter careful consideration. He'd been friendly enough until then, but the moment she'd offered to pay him for posing as Ulysses he'd gone as haughty as a duke. She'd been too set on obtaining her goal to pay his reaction proper attention, but now she could see that mentioning money had been a grave error in judgement.

Instead of offering to pay him for his assistance, perhaps she should have pointed out how the masquerade would benefit him. He was a visitor, after all, a stranger in a strange land, and surely he would need help establishing himself socially. She and her family might live in the country, but that didn't mean they weren't without influence. They had several friends amongst the gentry, and once he'd done his part posing as Ulysses, she could see he met the proper sort of people.

Yes, she thought, her lips curving in a pleased smile, that was what she'd do. She'd go to Mr. Canton at once, and tell him that in exchange for but one afternoon of his time, she would hold a tea in his honor and introduce him to all her friends. It was the perfect solution to both their problems, and her own cleverness delighted her. How could he possibly refuse?

She was brooding over how best to approach him, when her mother opened the door and hurried into the room. "Child, aren't you ready to leave yet?" she scolded, when she saw Penelope sitting before her dressing table. "The vicar is expecting us for tea, and you must hurry or we shall be shockingly late."

The mention of the tiresome young vicar made Penelope wince. "Not now, Mama, I beg of you. I have far more weighty concerns on my mind at the moment."

Her mother shook her head in disapproval, advancing on Penelope with a determined gleam in her eye. "Do not think you can wriggle out of our appointment that easily, young lady," she said, waggling an admonishing finger at Penelope. "You know full well we take tea with Mr. Downing the third Saturday of each month. Now stop your shilly-shallying, and go change. You can not possibly mean to leave this house dressed like that."

Penelope gazed down at her gown of gray sarcenet and frowned. "What is wrong with the way I am dressed?"

Her mother raised her eyes heavenward in a mute plea for divine patience. "I vow, there are times when you quite make me despair," she said, striding over to the wardrobe and throwing open the doors. "The greenest chit to draw breath would know that dress makes you look like a spinster at her last prayers. Wearing it is as good as declaring you have placed yourself on the shelf."

"I *have* placed myself on the shelf," Penelope reminded her. "I am four-and-twenty, and you said yourself it was unlikely I should ever wed."

"I know how old you are." Her mother's voice was muffled as she rummaged about in the wardrobe. "And what I said was that it was doubtful you should wed—and so you shan't—so long as you insist upon rigging yourself out in half-mourning. Now, what happened to that gown you wore to . . . ah, here it is." She emerged with a gown of cream and green-striped muslin clutched in her hands. "Wear this."

Penelope stared at the dress in dismay. It had been given to her by a distant relation, and while it was pretty enough, she didn't think it proper attire for a serious-minded young lady such as herself. The gown had come with a bonnet tied with sunny yellow ribbons, and in a matter of minutes her mother had unearthed that as well.

"This is much more the thing," she said approvingly, handing the items to Penelope. "Hurry and get out of that awful rag, and I'll ring for Jeanette to help you. We shall have to step lively if we wish to be on time."

Penelope made one last attempt to assert herself. "I appreciate your concern, mother, but I—"

"Penelope." Her mother gave her a look that withered the protest in her mouth. "I have put up with enough foolishness from you and your witless brother. I have endured your almost burning down the wash house with one of your experiments. I have even stood silently by while you defrauded a royal institution in the name of science. But I will not have you disgracing us all, dressing no better than a penniless governess! We shall take tea with Mr. Downing, and you will be dressed as befits a young lady. I shall be waiting downstairs."

Penelope stared after her, accepting defeat with a disgruntled sigh. Much as she would have liked to debate the matter, she knew her mama was right. She was already courting disgrace and disaster as it was, and it made little sense to risk causing more tattle when it could be so easily avoided. Just another example of how poorly her sex was used by the world, she thought, scowling as she reached for the rope pull.

"I am sorry, Mr. Canton, but there is nothing I can do to be of service to you," the vicar said, studying Daniel with wary disdain. "As I said, this is a family matter, and I am hardly free to discuss it with . . . outsiders. I am sure you understand."

Daniel's hands clenched in impotent fury at the pompous note in the younger man's nasal voice. He'd spent the past two days attempting to ferret out every scrap of information he could find, and his small store of patience was nearly at an end. He would have the answers he sought, he vowed silently, or the petulant dandy sitting before him would pay a heavy price.

"I will own my connection to the Burlingtons is tenuous," he said coldly, reaching deep inside himself for control, "but I am not an outsider. Now, you will do me the courtesy of answering my question. Was there an official investigation into either of my cousins' deaths, or was there not?"

The vicar's lips thinned in anger, and Daniel feared he may have overplayed his hand.

Then the vicar gave a loud sigh. "No, sir, there was not," he said, his irritation obvious. "Why should there be? People do die, you know."

"Indeed they do," Daniel responded in a tight voice. "But surely the deaths of two young men in such a relatively short period of time must have struck someone as odd. What of the present viscount? Was he not concerned about what happened to his brothers?"

The vicar gave another sigh. "The present viscount is but four-and-twenty, sir," he said, lifting his watch from his pocket and pointedly studying the time. "He was naturally distressed at losing his two remaining brothers, but I am told he has recovered from his grief. Now, I must insist that you leave. One of my parishioners and her daughter are coming for tea, and it would be ungentlemanly to keep them waiting. Good day."

Daniel bit back an impatient oath, accepting bitterly that there was little he could do. And at least he'd discovered there had been no investigation of Richard's and James's deaths, he thought, rising slowly to his feet. That was more than he'd known when he'd forced his way into the vicar's parlor an hour earlier.

"I thank you for your kindness," he said, inclining his head with mocking civility. "You have been most helpful."

The vicar's response was a prim sniff. "My housekeeper will see you out," he said coolly. "Good day."

Daniel turned toward the door and was reaching for the handle when it was suddenly pulled open, and he found himself face to face with Miss Grantham. There was a moment of shocked silence, then he collected himself and offered her a polite smile.

"Good afternoon, Miss Grantham," he said, sweeping his hat from his head. "How nice to see you again."

To his amusement her delicately hued cheeks suffused with color, and she looked as guilty as a child caught snatching pastries from a tray. "Mr. Canton!" she exclaimed, her hazel eyes wide with amazement. "Wh-what are you doing here?"

"I am calling on the good vicar," he replied, his gaze moving over her with reluctant admiration. Unlike the first time he had met her, she looked every inch the lady in her stylish gown and bonnet, and he recalled her claim to belong to a respectable family. At least she hadn't misled him on that account, he mused, noting the short, black-clad woman behind her who was regarding him with marked suspicion.

"Mrs. Grantham, I presume?" he said, taking care to keep any hint of laughter from his voice. "It is a pleasure to meet you."

"Indeed, sir?" came the frosty reply, as the older woman drew herself up with rigid disapproval. "And who might you be? I do not believe I have had the honor of your acquaintance."

"This is Mr. Canton, from America, Mama," Miss Grantham said, performing the introductions with undue haste. "We met the other day while I was at the churchyard. Mr.

Canton, allow me to introduce you to my mother, Mrs. Eustace Grantham.''

"Ma'am," Daniel bowed his head, hiding a smile from Mrs. Grantham's sharp gaze. It was easy to see how the daughter came by her shrewish temperament, he thought, taking an unholy delight in Miss Grantham's discomfiture. The past two days had been full of sorrow and anger, and he found an odd sort of relief in acting the scapegrace. He heard the vicar clearing his throat behind him, and realized it was time to beat a hasty retreat. He was about to make his goodbyes when Miss Grantham suddenly stepped in front of him.

"I was wondering if you had a chance yet to visit that bookshop I was telling you about," she said in a bright tone, her gaze desperate as she met his.

"I fear I have not yet had the opportunity," he answered slowly, wondering what the little devil was up to now. She had made no mention of a bookshop that he could recall.

"Oh, you really must make the effort." She laid a hand on his arm, and he could feel her fingers trembling. "It has an excellent selection of scientific journals I am sure you would find most interesting."

Daniel hesitated another moment, realizing she was attempting to arrange a rendezvous with him. "Perhaps I shall take the time, then," he said slowly, deciding he had nothing to lose by playing along with whatever rig she was running. "What was the name of that journal you recommended? I am afraid I can not recall it."

She sent him a grateful smile. "I will tell you again while I escort you to the door," she said, and led him out of the room, ignoring her mother's shocked gasp behind her. The moment they were in the narrow hallway she turned to face him.

"I must see you again," she said, casting the closed door a frantic look. "I know you rejected my suggestion, and I don't blame you, but there is something of great importance I should like to discuss with you. Alone," she added, stressing the word so that he would understand the seriousness of the situation.

Daniel stiffened in wariness. He may have been out of England for fifteen years, but he hadn't been gone so long that he'd forgotten how unbreakable were the strictures that governed society's behavior. Unmarried ladies did *not* arrange private meetings with strange gentlemen.

"I fear that is impossible, Miss Grantham," he said, deciding he'd had enough of her games. "I'm leaving for London tomorrow, and in any case, I do not feel it would be proper."

"Proper?" She flashed him a look rife with annoyance. "Don't be daft, sir! I haven't any designs on your virtue, I assure you. I want only the opportunity to speak with you. Will you meet me, or will you not?"

Daniel bristled, aware his masculinity had just been impugned. He knew he should tell the little vixen no, and yet he could not help but be a little curious. "Where is this bookshop you mentioned?" he asked, reaching an abrupt decision.

"It is on the next street, across from a small square," she said, her shoulders relaxing in relief. "Wait for me, and I shall meet you there in an hour. *Please*."

The desperation in her voice added to his curiosity. "Very well, then. But," he added before she could offer him her thanks, "I must warn you that if you are plotting to trick me into helping you, I shall be most displeased. I do not take kindly to being manipulated."

"This is no trick," she promised, already turning away. "An hour, Mr. Canton, and I promise you shall have the answers you seek."

Daniel watched her dart back into the room, his eyes narrowing with thought. He had to be mad to even think of involving himself in her machinations, when he had so much else on his plate just now. On the other hand . . . His lips curled in a wry smile as he contemplated the matter. Trying to deal with Miss Grantham was preferable to brooding over his brothers' mysterious deaths. And their deaths *were* mysterious, he decided with a sigh. Of that he was more convinced than ever, and it was a mystery he was committed to solving regardless of the cost to himself.

3

Placating her mama and slipping away to meet Mr. Canton proved difficult but not impossible, and it was only a few minutes past the appointed time when Penelope entered the bookshop. As she'd hoped, the shop appeared deserted, which was one of the reasons she'd chosen it for their rendezvous. The other reason was that the owner was a good friend, and she knew he could be counted upon to hold his tongue. Not that she really needed to worry on that score, she thought, pushing open the door. Even the most dedicated gossip would be hard-pressed to find anything untoward in two young people encountering each other in a bookshop.

The bell gave a familiar tinkle as she entered, and a quick glance about showed she was quite alone. She was beginning to fear Mr. Canton had turned craven, when he suddenly appeared from behind the wooden door that separated the front of the shop from the private quarters in the rear.

"So you came," he drawled, advancing on her with a mocking smile. "I was wondering if you would."

She bristled at the implication she could be so chicken-hearted. "Of course I came," she said, scowling up at him. "This was my idea, you know."

"So it was," he agreed, not stopping until he was standing directly before her. "Now perhaps you'd be so good as to tell me what the devil you are up to. And before you begin, I think it only fair to warn you that I have no patience for games. If you wish something I should appreciate your saying so, rather than wasting my time with a lot of tiresome dramatics.''

His implacable attitude gave Penelope pause, and she wondered uneasily if perhaps she'd made an error in judgement in selecting him. During the ride to the vicarage her mama had mentioned the possibility of hiring an actor to impersonate Ulysses, but she'd rejected the idea as untenable. Now she wasn't so certain.

If a man could be trained to memorize Shakespeare's scribblings, perhaps he could be taught to memorize her theories as well. At least they made sense, and she would be close at hand to cover in obvious gaps in his knowledge. Certainly that would be a better choice than a sardonic American who held entirely too high an opinion of himself, she thought.

Then she gave her head a mental shake. It was a poor scientist indeed who abandoned a promising experiment after one or two minor setbacks. Mr. Canton was still her best chance of resolving her present difficulties, and she would be beyond foolish to throw that away merely because the man was a trifle overbearing. She need only suffer his company a few hours, and then they would be shed of each other. The notion soothed her overwrought nerves.

''I was wondering, sir, if you have thought at all about my suggestion that you pose as my brother,'' she said, trying to sound cool and in control. She wished he wasn't standing quite so close to her. She found she disliked having him loom over her, as much as she disliked his arrogance.

He folded his arms across his chest in obvious challenge. ''Your offer to *pay* me, do you mean?'' he asked, his green eyes narrowing. ''I can not say that I have.''

So she was right and her offer of money had offended him, she thought in delight. ''I did not mean to be offensive,'' she said, deciding he might be more amenable if she showed a hint of penitence. ''I should have realized at once that you are a gentleman, and of course wouldn't have dreamed of accepting payment for helping a lady.'' She gave him a cautious glance to see how her apology was received.

He met her gaze with a mocking smile. "Perhaps it was the amount that was offered rather than the offer itself I found offensive," he replied in that same maddening drawl. "Twenty pounds might seem a great fortune to you, but it is hardly enough to tempt me into participating in such a ridiculous charade."

Penelope could scarce believe such cheek. She'd heard Americans were shrewd businessmen, but she had never imagined anything like this! She shot him a furious glare. "And how much would it take to tempt you, then?" she demanded crossly. An actor was looking better with each passing second.

His smile vanished. "There is no amount of money that would make me willing to sell myself," he said curtly. "Now, what is it you wish to discuss? As I said, I'm leaving for London tomorrow, and I have little time to waste."

Penelope nibbled on her lower lip, trying to decide what she should do. It didn't help that he was standing so close to her, making her uncomfortably aware of his sheer size. He'd discarded his hat and gloves, but he was still wearing his cloak. The artois coat was in the first crack of fashion, and she found herself wondering if his broad shoulders were the result of nature or merely an illusion created by the coat's many capes. She strongly suspected it was the former. He didn't strike her as the type to resort to artifice.

"Miss Grantham?" His deep voice interrupted her musings, and she glanced up to find him watching her with those narrowed, jewel-colored eyes. "I am waiting."

"When I first mentioned your posing as Ulysses, I only said how such a deception would benefit me," she said, deciding it best to get the thing over with as swiftly as possible. "What I didn't say was how it might benefit you as well."

He jerked his head back in surprise. "Me?" he repeated, looking genuinely puzzled. "How could posing as your brother be of any benefit to me?"

"It's not so much the posing. Rather, it's what I am willing to do in exchange for your help that would be the benefit."

There was a short silence as he continued watching her. "And precisely what is it you're willing to do?"

Penelope hesitated, her cheeks pinking with embarrassment

at the unspoken innuendo in his words. "I—I could introduce you to my friends," she stammered, confidence in her scheme wavering. "You said you don't know anyone in England, and I thought perhaps you might enjoy meeting people.

"England's not like America, you know," she added when his expression remained unchanged. "Ours is a rigid, and, I fear, rather insular society. Unless one has been properly introduced, it can be difficult to establish friendships. At least, I have always found it so." She gave a self-deprecating laugh, wishing miserably that she'd never started this conversation.

He remained silent for several moments, his gaze never leaving her face. "Out of curiosity, is there really a Mr. Grantham, or is that the *nom de guerre* you have selected for yourself?" he asked at last, his deep voice giving away nothing of his thoughts.

"Both," Penelope replied, relaxing slightly when she realized he was listening to her, rather than dismissing her out of hand. "I do have a brother named Ulysses, but he is the farthest thing from a scientist one may imagine."

"I see." Daniel's lips twitched at her bluntness. "That explains why you haven't solicited his help. Or have you?" He gave her a questioning look.

"Good heavens, no," she answered, shuddering at the very thought. "Please do not misunderstand me. I love Ulysses dearly, but I would have better luck trying to pass off one of the royal dukes as a scientist than I would Ulysses. He fancies himself a knight of old, when he is not playing at being an invalid, and I fear he would be worse than useless."

Her fervent words made him chuckle, but his amusement quickly faded. He met her gaze somberly. "Why me?"

Penelope didn't pretend to misunderstand him. "You are intelligent, well-spoken, and best of all, you'll soon be leaving England," she said, listing all the reasons he was so perfect for her needs. "You can impersonate Ulysses and return to your home with no one ever the wiser."

He gave a quick nod and then frowned. "But what of your brother? He has lived here all his life. Surely he must know several people who would be certain to remark on the difference in our appearances. Unless by some odd coincidence we look alike?'' he added, studying her curiously.

She gazed up at his handsome face and shook her head. ''Ulysses has my coloring, and he's not nearly so large. I mean,'' she amended, blushing when he raised an eyebrow, ''he isn't as tall and muscular as you. And as for his knowing many people, I doubt that will be a problem. My father didn't believe in formal education, so Ulysses was educated at home. He's been a recluse for many years, and he shuns people whenever possible. He says they give him the headache,'' she added, apologizing for her brother's eccentricities with a self-conscious shrug.

There was another silence as he stood watching her. ''You said your work has met with some success,'' he said, his gaze resting on her face. ''Precisely how well-known is Ulysses?''

The question made her squirm. ''Among other scientists I should say he is rather well-known,'' she admitted, wondering how much she could tell him without scaring him away. ''My last experiment involving electrical properties received some notice from The Royal Institution.''

Daniel turned and walked away, his back to her as he stared out the shop's bowed window. ''Let us assume this insane scheme of yours has the slightest chance of succeeding,'' he said, gazing out at the deserted street. ''How will you explain that I know next to nothing about electrical properties? I'll have to do more than smile and make my bows if you are to keep your stipend, won't I?'' He turned around and nailed her with a piercing look.

His acuity made her more uncomfortable than ever, and she shot him a resentful look. ''I've already thought of that.'' She hoped she didn't sound as petulant as she felt. ''No one will expect you to conduct the experiments yourself, you know. You have only to read from the notes I will prepare, and I shall do everything else.

''It *will* work,'' she insisted, when he looked unconvinced. ''I've already established that I am Ulysses's assistant, and no one will so much as blink to see me helping you.''

''All right.''

Penelope frowned at his blunt reply. ''I beg your pardon?''

"All right, I shall help you," he said, meeting her stunned gaze with stolid composure.

At first she couldn't believe the evidence of her own ears, then relief flooded through her. "Oh, Mr. Canton, thank you!" she exclaimed, sending him a brilliant smile. "How shall I ever be able to repay you? I—"

"With certain provisions, of course."

The unyielding edge in his voice extinguished her brief flicker of joy, and she gaped at him in astonishment. "See here, sir," she began indignantly, only to have him shake his head.

"No, Miss Grantham, *you* see here," he said, returning to stand in front of her. "You are the one who sought my help, and if you wish that help you would be wise to agree to my terms."

Such blatant despotism infuriated Penelope beyond all bearing, but beneath her fury was a realization that he was right. She needed him far more than he needed her, and that meant he held the upper hand. But someday . . . she vowed, swallowing her pride with considerable difficulty. "And pray, sir, what are your terms?" she asked, forcing the question past clenched teeth.

"First I want it clear that I am in charge," he said, the hard cast of his face making it obvious he would brook no opposition. "I am seasoned enough to know that in any endeavor there can be but one leader, and I mean to be that leader. You'll take your instructions from me, and if I tell you to do something you'll do it, and without endless arguments and questions. Understood?"

Penelope felt as if a supposedly inert compound had just exploded in her face. Of all the reactions she'd envisioned, it never occurred to her that he would commandeer the entire operation. "But this was my idea!" she protested. "You simply can't step in and take over!"

"Can I not?" The smile he gave her was as sharp as a knife. "What will you do if I refuse?"

Frustration held Penelope mute, and she glared at him in impotent fury.

"It won't be so bad," he soothed, taking her silence for

acquiescence. "I shan't be any more dictatorial than any other brother, which is only proper when you think about it. To the world I shall be your elder brother, and all I ask is that you accord me the same respect and obedience you would show him. Are we agreed?"

Penelope paused, an evil plan forming in her mind. "The same respect?" she asked, a crafty smile curving her lips.

"The same," he agreed, crossing his arms and looking stern.

She pretended to consider the matter. "I suppose your suggestion is not without merit," she said slowly. "And as it is for a good cause, I daresay there is no reason why I shouldn't treat you as I do Ulysses. Very well." She tilted back her head and gave him her sweetest smile. "We are agreed."

Her victory was short-lived.

"And naturally I shall pay for everything."

Penelope's jaw dropped in astonishment. "But, sir, that is most improper! I shall be the one who will benefit most, and—"

"And my pockets are far deeper than yours," he finished for her, reaching out to cup her chin in his hand. "Consider it my contribution to scientific advancement," he said softly, his thumb brushing lightly over her jaw. "Come, Penelope, what do you say?"

At first Penelope had no breath with which to respond. She wasn't sure which disconcerted her more: that Mr. Canton had used her given name without permission, or that he was touching her in what could only be termed a caress. It was the first time any man had ever presumed to touch her so intimately, and it stunned her to discover she didn't find the sensation as distasteful as propriety dictated she should. Flushing in confusion, she took a quick step backward.

"You must know I can not give you an answer this very minute," she said, scrambling to gather her wits. "I shall need time to consider your offer, and naturally I must discuss it with my mother."

"You may take all the time you need, so long as I have your answer by tomorrow."

She jerked up her head in alarm. "Tomorrow?"

He gave her a cool smile. "I believe I mentioned I was leaving for London at that time," he said smoothly. "I see no reason why I should delay my departure. You'll either come with me, or you will not."

Several pithy remarks sprang to mind, but Penelope managed to swallow most of them. "Arrogant devil," she muttered, and felt a sharp sense of relief when the bell above the door gave a merry tinkle. Now she could quit his presence without giving him the satisfaction of thinking he had routed her.

"Nonsense," he responded, his smile widening at her acerbic accusation. "I am merely being firm. And firmness, I am sure you will agree, is a desirable attribute in an older brother." He took a discreet step back from her and gave her a low bow.

"Good day, Miss Grantham. You may send word to me at The Blue Jar once you have reached your decision."

"I knew this would happen some day," Mrs. Grantham moaned, her vial of smelling salts clutched in her hand. "I told your papa allowing you to read all those tiresome books would have a detrimental effect on your senses, but he would not listen to me. No one ever listens to me!"

"Really, Mama, don't you think you are doing it a shade too brown?" Penelope eyed her mother with exasperation. "There's nothing wrong with my intellectual abilities."

"You have the brass to tell me that, after saying you have engaged Mr. Canton to pose as Ulysses?" Mrs. Grantham demanded, taking a restorative sniff of her salts. "Your wits have gone begging! It's all that infernal electricity you've been studying, I'll wager. Did I not say no good would come from tinkering with nature?"

Penelope closed her eyes wearily, striving for patience as she pinched the bridge of her nose. As a scientist she knew that a straightforward approach was best when presenting a recommendation, but as a daughter she understood a less direct approach was ofttimes better. Especially when one was dealing with an overly emotional female like her mama.

"I fail to see why you are so upset," she muttered, heartily sick of people expressing doubt in her sanity. "*You* are the one who suggested we engage the services of an actor. What is so very different in allowing Mr. Canton to perform the same service? At least he is a gentleman, and we may count upon his word not to betray us."

Her mother shot Penelope a censorious glare. "He is an American," she corrected sternly, her lips thinning in displeasure. "It is hardly the same thing at all."

"Mama—"

"Besides," Mrs. Grantham added, her expression growing mulish, "he is far too old to be Ulysses. Why, he is positively aged!"

Penelope thought of the vital, virile man she had left in the bookshop and repressed a grin. "I'm not sure how old he is," she confessed, recalling the lines etched in his tanned cheeks, "but I'd hardly go so far as to call him *aged*. He can not be above five-and-thirty."

"And I am scarce above forty!" her mother shot back, scowling indignantly. "Would you have people think I was increasing when I was scarce out of the cradle? No, it simply will not do."

"You are forty-nine, and Ulysses will be thirty in less than a year," Penelope corrected. "Besides, Mr. Canton is supposed to be Ulysses, and if anyone should be so rude as to mention the matter, he can tell them he is thirty and be done with it. Why should it matter?"

Mrs. Grantham surged to her feet. "It matters, you foolish girl, because Ulysses is . . . well, Ulysses, but your Mr. Canton is very much the man. If people take me for his mama, they will think me as old as Methuselah!" And she burst into noisy tears.

Too late, Penelope understood the reasons behind her mother's objections, and rushed to repair the damage she had done. "Nonsense, Mama," she soothed, giving her mother a tender hug and lowering her gently to the settee. "How could anyone looking at you think such a foolish thing? Why, you look scarce old enough to be my mama!"

"I—I was so looking forward to visiting London," her mother sniffed, dabbing at her eyes with her handkerchief. "I always wanted to go, but your papa would not take me. Now if I go I shall have to sit on the dowager's bench, and—and wear c-caps!'' She sobbed even harder.

It took quite a while and two glasses of Madeira, but Penelope was eventually able to overcome her mother's objections. She even told her of Mr. Canton's generous offer to fund the expedition, and as she expected, her mother refused to even consider taking advantage of such largesse. His intention to rule the roost as the head of the family, however, did meet with her whole-hearted approval.

"Well, of course he should,'' her mother said, brightening at the news. "A fine son he would be if he expected his mama or sister to see to such things.''

"But Mama, he is not your son,'' Penelope protested, stung by her mother's defection to the enemy's camp. "He is but playing a part. I know we aren't paying him for his assistance, but in a manner of speaking he is our servant. It is for us to tell him what to do, not the other way around.''

"Don't be ungrateful, child,'' her mother rebuked, looking stern. "It is very good of Mr. Canton to treat us so kindly. Now, when did you say he wished to leave?''

"Tomorrow,'' Penelope said, accepting defeat with a heavy sigh. "He said I am to send him word at The Blue Jar once we have decided to accept his terms.''

"Tomorrow!'' Her mother leapt to her feet a second time. "Well, what are you waiting for?'' she demanded when Penelope gaped up at her. "Send him a note at once, and tell him we shall place ourselves at his disposal!''

"But—''

"Penelope,'' Mrs. Grantham gazed down at her in obvious annoyance, "must you question everything I say? Just send Mr. Canton the note, then begin packing at once. We shall have to work all night if we are to be ready in time.''

Penelope mentally lifted her hands in surrender, accepting that there was nothing else she could do. Mr. Canton had won yet another round, and resistance at this point would be useless. But her own time would come, Penelope promised herself, rising to go in search of pen and paper.

And when that time came, she thought, dipping the quill in

the inkwell, she would take great delight in seeing that he paid a dear price for his temerity. Another thing the study of science had taught her was that in the end, patience was often more important than intelligence. She had only to wait, and then she would take her vengeance. The thought cheered Penelope so much, she was even able to sound grateful as she penned her acceptance.

He'd lost his bloody mind, Daniel decided ruefully, leaning back in his chair to enjoy his glass of port. Surely only a man completely bereft of reason would allow himself to become party to so preposterous a charade. He knew he'd have to tread carefully if he had any hopes of succeeding, and even then, he acknowledged, the whole thing was likely to end in disaster. Especially when one had an unpredictable female like Miss Grantham as a confederate.

When she'd first renewed her offer he had been fully prepared to reject her out of hand, not wanting to involve himself in another person's problems. Yet the more she talked, the more he realized that posing as her brother presented him with the perfect opportunity to investigate his brothers' deaths. Not only would it remove the problem of establishing an identity for himself, but it also presented him with an *entree* to society.

Miss Grantham had been right when she said English society was insular. Even in a tiny village like Bibury, his apparent lack of ties to a social class had proven a distinct barrier. The few members of the gentry he'd met had treated him with wary politeness, uncertain if he was one of them or a member of the lower orders, and he knew that in London it would be even worse.

If he clung to his present masquerade, that of an American visiting the land of his parent's birth, his access to the *ton* would be severely limited. Without connections, he hadn't a hope in Hades of investigating what had happened to Richard and James. But as Ulysses Grantham, a well-bred young scientist of some renown, he would be granted *carte blanche* to even the highest level of society. He could move about freely, asking as many questions as he pleased, and no one would ever think to question either his identity or his motives.

If there was any flaw he could detect, it was that he would be forced to deal with Miss Grantham and her willful temperament. That was why he'd insisted on assuming control—knowing that given half a chance, she'd run roughshod over him without a bat of her pretty lashes. He'd have enough to deal with, without worrying about what new mischief his supposed sister had fallen into, and he wanted it understood that if she wanted his help, she would do as she was told.

At least her mama would be there to keep her in line, he reflected, taking another sip of the sweet wine. Not that she'd done a stellar job of the task to date, mind. It was plain that Miss Grantham had been allowed to run free far too long, and that it was time a firmer hand took control of the reins.

Thinking of Mrs. Grantham made him pause, and he wondered how she felt about having him as a son. The Lord knew his own mother had never found the prospect particularly pleasing, and he hoped she wouldn't be similarly disappointed. Likely she would not, he decided with a quiet chuckle. If the poor lady had survived having Miss Grantham as a daughter, it was obvious she was made of sterner stuff.

The letter from Miss Grantham arrived just as he was setting out. He scanned the note, pleased to see that he'd achieved the important goal of winning Miss Grantham's grudging cooperation. Not that he truly believed she meant to keep her word, he thought, a wry smile touching his lips. His ersatz sister was too much like him to let his high-handed behavior go unpunished, and he would have to keep on his toes once they were in London.

It was approaching the dinner hour as he left the inn, so the shops had already closed for the day. He'd been in the village long enough that his appearance warranted no more than the occasional stare, and no one called out to him as he rode out of the village toward the churchyard. In less than a quarter-hour he was standing in front of his brothers' graves, his head bent as he studied the headstones.

What had happened? he wondered bleakly, feeling the fresh sting of tears in his eyes. Why had his brothers died so young, and so close to each other? He'd asked dozens of questions, and for each one answered, a hundred more rose to take their place. Nothing made sense, and beneath his frustration, the awful guilt that nibbled at his soul grew ever stronger—the guilt that, had he not sailed off for America in defiance of his father, he might have been able to prevent those headstones.

"Good evening, my lord."

Daniel whirled around, and found himself confronting a face from his past. The man was tall, with a thin patch of hair, once bright red, that had faded to a dull, rusty gray. It had been well past a decade since he'd last seen those keen blue eyes, but Daniel recognized his father's steward at once.

"Polson?" he gasped, accepting in a flash that attempting to deny his identity would be futile. Polson had always possessed the uncanny ability to see past any subterfuge.

An explosion of wrinkles burst about the older man's eyes as he smiled. "Aye, lad, 'tis me." His deep voice rang with the music of his Irish birth. "And might I say, you are looking remarkably well for a man who has been in his grave long these past fifteen years."

Daniel didn't know how to respond at first, but the longer he stared at the other man, the more certain his conviction became. "You knew I was alive, didn't you?"

Polson nodded, his expression grim. "I told your father it was a mad thing he was doing," he said. "I warned him that you had but to come back and all would know the truth, but he would not listen. He never listened. 'Twas a trait the two of you shared," he added, his eyes meeting Daniel's.

Daniel felt the sharp stab of an old pain. "He never listened to me, that much is certain," he said bitterly, turning back to study the graves with unseeing eyes. "I wonder now what would have happened if he had. Perhaps . . ."

"Perhaps nothing, lad," Polson said quietly. "Your parents' deaths were God's will, and your being here would not have altered a thing. Don't let yourself long for that which cannot be changed. 'Tis a fool's game, and difficult though you were, you were never a fool."

Daniel thrust his hand through his hair, not trusting himself to speak. "My parents' deaths, I accept," he said at last, his voice ragged with emotion. "But not Richard's. Not James's.

They were too young, and the ways they died too puzzling to be believed. Am I the only one to see this?''

"No, my lord, you are not.''

Daniel raised his head at that. "What do you mean?''

"I never believed young Richard would take a half-wild horse out for a moonlight ride, be he drunk or sober. And the last I saw of Master James, he was in the rarest good health you could imagine. That was four days before he died, and not a trace of fever did I detect in him.''

Daniel's hands clenched into tight fists. "Then why didn't you demand an inquest be held?'' he demanded furiously. "When I asked him, that dolt of a vicar said one had never been ordered!''

Polson gave a bitter laugh. "You've been gone from England too long, sir, if you're thinking the magistrates would listen to the likes of me,'' he said, his lips twisting in a travesty of a smile. "They'd not hear a word of what I had to say—not with a fine lord standing there assuring them all was well.''

"What fine lord?'' Daniel demanded, having not heard this bit of information before. He'd always assumed James had died alone, with no one except the servants to tend him.

"Lord Haworth.'' Polson all but spat out the name. "He and Master James had become thick as two inkleweavers in the months before he died, and he was here when the sickness came over the viscount. His lordship insisted the lad be treated by his personal physician, and he even sent his own carriage down to London to fetch the man here. Master James died before the doctor arrived.''

"Haworth?'' Daniel exclaimed, a deadly anger beginning to burn in his belly. "Wasn't he Richard's host?''

"Aye, George Henry Alistair, the Marquess of Haworth, and a right proper swell he is, too,'' Polson said with another harsh laugh. "He said he always felt to blame for young Richard dying, and that was why he was so set on befriending Master James.''

"And where is this Lord Haworth now?'' Daniel asked. "In London?''

"Like as not,'' Polson shrugged. "I heard his fortunes were in decline and he was on the hang for a rich wife.''

Daniel smiled grimly. He'd learned long ago that knowing an enemy's weakness made him easier to defeat, and as of this moment, he considered Haworth the most deadly of enemies. There was just one thing left that puzzled him.

"You keep calling me my lord," he said slowly, fixing Polson with a piercing look. "Why?"

Polson looked momentarily taken aback. "Why?" he repeated incredulously. "Why, because, God love you, sir, that is who you are. With Richard and James dead without heirs, you are next in line to the title. You are the new viscount."

4

"*The viscount?*" Daniel stared at Polson in disbelief. "How can this be? What of Andrew?"

"Andrew is eleven years your junior," Polson reminded him gently. "You are the eldest surviving son, and under the laws of primogeniture, the title falls to you. That is why you've come home, 'tis it not?" he added, when Daniel remained silent.

Daniel could only shake his head, too ill to speak. He'd been so preoccupied with learning the details of what had happened to Richard and James, that the matter of the title had simply slipped his mind. He'd assumed he'd been disinherited long ago, and that the title had naturally fallen to Andrew. Now he wasn't certain what to believe.

"I came back to make peace with what remained of my family," he said heavily, turning from Polson to lay his hand on Richard's stone. "Word reached me that both Richard and James had died, and I realized it was time to return. I'd meant to come before now, but . . ." He closed his eyes as a wave of bitterness washed over him.

"You'll be going to London to see Lord Burlington . . . Master Andrew, then?" Polson asked, watching him curiously.

Daniel opened his eyes and sent Polson a warning look. "Andrew is still Lord Burlington."

"But my lord—"

39

"No," he interrupted, straightening to his full height. "I told you, the title is Andrew's. You forget that as far as the rest of the world is concerned, Daniel Warfield is dead, and that is the way I prefer it. For now," he added, his tone grim.

Polson remained silent a long moment, his expression revealing nothing of his thoughts. "That explains why you've taken a room under a name not your own," he said, nodding his head in understanding. "I'll admit I wondered if you were up to your old tricks again."

Recalling some of the stunts he'd pulled in his salad days, Daniel couldn't take offense at the steward's wry observation. He was about to say as much when something Polson said made him frown. "How did you know I was here?" he asked.

"One of the lads you spoke with is seeing one of our maids, and he mentioned you'd been asking questions," Polson said with a shrug. "I saw you leaving the bookshop this afternoon, and followed you back to the inn."

Daniel didn't like the sound of that. "Why didn't you just come up and talk to me?" he demanded with a scowl, annoyed at the thought that he'd been shadowed as if he were a desperate criminal.

"I didn't want to approach you until I was certain you weren't out to make mischief," Polson admitted bluntly. "You've been gone for fifteen years, and without so much as a letter the whole time. What else was I to think but that you were here for some nefarious purpose?"

Daniel gave a harsh laugh. "I didn't write because my father made it plain no correspondence from me would be welcome," he said, remembering how deeply that had cut him at the time. "He told me that unless I abandoned my folly and gave in to his wishes, I would be cut off from the family. That is why I'm so surprised to learn I am in line for the title. Are you quite certain I wasn't disinherited?"

"A dead son doesn't need to be disinherited," Polson returned, gesturing at the memorial Daniel had seen that first day. "When the papers printed the news two ships bound for America were lost in a storm, your father saw it as an answer to his prayers. He told everyone you'd been on board the first of them, and declared you dead. The family gave you a proper year of mourning, you'll be pleased to know," he said in an obvious attempt at humor.

The hypocrisy that his father could mourn a dead son, rather than welcoming a live one, made Daniel feel ill. "How reassuring," he said, making no attempt to hide his rancor. "I'd have thought they'd have held a ball instead. But of course, that would have caused tongues to wag, would it not?"

"Your brothers genuinely mourned you," Polson said, moving to stand beside him. "Especially Richard. He and your father quarrelled over it often, and Richard let him know he considered your death his fault. They were never close after that."

Daniel felt a painful lump gather in his throat. "What happened, Polson?" he asked rawly. "How could Richard have died in an accident both of us know should never have occurred?"

"I do not know, sir."

Daniel appreciated his honesty. "Neither do I, Polson. But I swear on both my brothers's graves, I shall learn the truth. That is why I'm going to London."

Polson studied Daniel's face a long moment. "Will you be staying at Cavendish Square?"

Daniel thought of the elegant mansion his family maintained in the city, and shook his head. "It would be rather difficult to appear on Andrew's doorstep when I am supposed to be dead," he replied wryly. "I wouldn't want to frighten the poor lad to death; then I truly would be stuck with the wretched title."

"Then you don't intend going as yourself?" Polson asked, ignoring the last of Daniel's remark.

Daniel hesitated a moment before responding. Miss Grantham hadn't sworn him to secrecy, precisely, but he was reluctant to discuss her deception with anyone, even Polson.

"I mean to go as one of your neighbors, a Mr. Ulysses Grantham," he replied warily. "Do you know him?"

Polson frowned and rocked back on his heels. "I cannot say as I do," he admitted, "although I'll own the name is somewhat familiar. He is a neighbor, you say?"

"If his sister is to be believed, he lives not far from here. She said he was a bit of a recluse."

Polson's brow cleared as if by magic. "Ah, the scientific gentleman! Aye, he lives not far from the village with his mother and sister. But why would you want to pose as him?" he added, frowning again. "I've heard he's mad as a March hare, and goes about in a suit of armor when he's not conducting those experiments of his."

"Posing as a slightly balmy young scientist serves my purposes better than going as myself. I've earned his sister's agreement to go along with the charade, and in exchange I shall provide her and her mother with a few weeks in the city," Daniel replied, deciding he'd already said enough on the subject. "I trust you may be relied upon to hold your tongue? It would be disastrous for all concerned were my true identity to become known."

"Master Daniel!" Polson drew himself up rigidly. "I've spent my life working for your family. You can not mean to question my loyalty now!"

"No, Polson, I do not." Daniel was ashamed of himself for having offended a man who had always treated him fairly. "But you must realize I am not the only one involved. Miss Grantham's good name could be tarnished if word of this should leak out."

"You may rely on me, sir," Polson assured him with pride.

"Good," Daniel said quietly. "Because there is something else I would ask of you."

Polson looked uncertain. "And what might that be?"

"It's two things, actually. First, I don't want you writing Andrew and telling him I am alive and back in England. I'll do so eventually," he added when it looked as it Polson would protest, "but in my own good time, and under my own terms."

"And the second thing?"

"I want you to use your influence to get the Granthams and myself vouchers to Almacks."

"Almacks!" Polson turned an alarming shade of red. But sir—"

"I know you have connections," Daniel interrupted, ignoring the steward's sputtering protests. "All I ask is that you use them to secure the vouchers for us."

"Is there anything else? Mayhap 'tis an introduction to the prince you'll be needing?" Polson asked ironically.

Daniel's smile was as cold as the marble that surrounded him. "I am glad you mentioned that," he said smoothly. "Listen carefully; this is what I have in mind . . ."

Despite her mother's tearful prediction they would never be ready in time, Penelope had both of them packed and ready to leave at the appointed hour. Of course, it meant going without sleep and enduring Ulysses's misguided attempts to help, but still she managed . . . barely. She was packing the last box of scientific instruments when the giggling maid ushered Mr. Canton into her laboratory.

"I trust you are ready to leave," he said, advancing briskly toward her. "The team is growing restive and—" His voice broke off as he stared at her. "What the deuce is that?"

Penelope gazed fondly at the large box she was holding in her hand. "It is a Cruickshank battery," she said, smiling with pride. It had taken her three years to afford the device, and she wasn't about to leave it behind for Ulysses to tinker with.

Daniel approached her with all the caution of a man creeping up to a sleeping tiger. "What does it do?" he asked dubiously, reaching out to stroke one of the metal plates soldered together and sealed in the narrow box.

"It's a machine that produces and stores an electrical charge. I use it in my work," she replied, pleased by his interest.

"Are you taking it with you?"

Penelope wasn't sure what to make of his question. "I'd thought to," she replied carefully, her grip tightening on the wooden case. "Do you have any objections?"

He lifted his head from his perusal of the box, a slow smile spreading across his face. "So long as you promise to instruct me in its use, ma'am, you may bring the entire room with you, if that is your pleasure," he drawled huskily, his green eyes dancing as they met hers.

His teasing reply and slow smile took Penelope by surprise,

and she was annoyed to feel herself blushing. "Well, perhaps I shan't take the *entire* room, Mr. Canton," she said, hiding behind a light laugh. "There are a few other instruments I should like to bring, but—"

"Daniel," he interrupted, reaching out and plucking the battery from her hands. "If we are to be brother and sister, you had best accustom yourself to using my Christian name."

Penelope thought about that for a moment. "If we were truly brother and sister, I would be calling you Ulysses," she pointed out.

"Not if you wish me to answer, you won't," he said with a mock shudder. "However did the poor lad come to be saddled with such a name? Is it a family name?"

Penelope shook her head. "He came by his name the same way I came by mine," she said, moving away from him to remove a Leyden jar from a shelf. "Papa's favorite book was *The Odyssey*, and nothing would do but that he name us after the main characters. Had I had another brother, he would have been called Ajax."

Daniel gave a low chuckle. "Ajax isn't so bad a name," he said with a reminiscent grin. "I had a cousin named Ajax, and he was a capital fellow, as I recall."

Penelope was momentarily distracted by the confession. This was the first time since their meeting he'd mentioned his family, and it occurred to her how very little she actually knew of him.

"Where does your cousin live?" she asked, studying him from beneath her lashes as she finished packing the jar. "Is he English, or American like yourself?"

"Neither," he replied curtly, a blank mask sliding over his face as he set down the battery. "He died several years ago."

"I'm sorry," Penelope said gently, regretting touching on such an obviously painful memory. "What of your other cousin? Will you be calling on him while we're in London?"

"What other cousin?" he asked, scowling at her in confusion.

"Lord Burlington," she reminded him. "That first day we met, I believe I mentioned he lives in town."

His countenance grew even grimmer. "I haven't yet decided

what I shall do," he said, pulling his watch from his pocket and studying it with marked impatience. "It is almost ten o'clock," he said, snapping the watch case closed and returning it to his pocket. "I'll give you another quarter hour to complete your packing, and then we will be leaving. I wouldn't suggest you keep me waiting, else you may find yourself left behind." He walked out before Penelope could think of a suitable rejoinder.

Despite the inauspicious beginning, the journey to London was relatively pleasant for Penelope and her mother. This was the first time they had travelled in such an elegant coach, and the soft leather seats and padded velvet sides did much to soothe her temper. She even unbent enough to offer Daniel instruction in the use of the battery and friction machine, and was delighted when he caught on at once. The questions he asked were both intelligent and incisive, and by the time they reached the outskirts of the city she had completely forgotten the incident in her laboratory.

On the journey to London, Daniel and her mother haggled over who would be responsible for the expenses they would be incurring while in the city. Daniel renewed his insistence that he be allowed to stake them, an offer her mother adamantly refused to even consider. Penelope watched the battle in amused silence, impressed at the way her mother bent the imperious Mr. Canton to her will with a sweet smile and a firm shake of her head. It was something she would have to remember in the event she and her "brother" should ever clash again, she thought, her eyes sparkling with suppressed laughter.

They broke for a quick tea at a small inn, and after their journey renewed, Daniel casually mentioned that he'd rented a small house for the Season and that he hoped they would find it to their liking. This cavalier description in no way prepared Penelope for the sumptuous mansion awaiting them when their carriage finally rumbled to a halt on South Audley Street.

"*This* is the little townhouse you have rented?" she gasped, feeling every inch the country bumpkin as she stood on the sidewalk gaping up at the brick and marble edifice.

"Yes, it is," he replied, helping her mother from the carriage before turning to frown at her. "Why? Is there something wrong with it?"

"Wrong?" She bit back the hysterical laughter rising in her throat. "No, not at all. It is just I wasn't expecting anything so . . . so large," she finished lamely.

He gave an indifferent shrug, dismissing the house's opulence in a manner that made her even more nervous. "I wrote my man of business to find me something respectable," he said, sliding his hand beneath her elbow and urging her forward. "If you do not feel it will suit, I am sure he can us find something else."

"Nonsense, Ulysses," Mrs. Grantham said, falling easily into the habit of addressing him by her son's name. "The house is fine, I assure you, and I daresay we shall all be merry as crickets."

The door to the house was thrown open before they had even reached the steps, and what seemed like an army of servants was lined up in the black-and-white-marbled hallway to receive them. The butler, a regal individual named Carlyle, performed the necessary introductions, and by the time he was finished Penelope's head was reeling with shock. She felt as if she was in the middle of some fantastical dream, and her hand was trembling as she reached out to grab Daniel's arm.

"I must speak with you," she said urgently, her gaze searching his face. "When you insisted you would be providing our lodgings, I never expected anything like this! It is too much; you will beggar yourself!"

A slight smile touched his eyes at her frantic tone. "Do not concern yourself," he said softly, giving her hand a reassuring pat. "I am far from a poor man. I can easily afford this house and the running of it, I promise you."

"But—"

He silenced her by laying a gloved finger against her lips. "It will be all right," he assured her, his gaze holding hers. "Trust me, Penelope, I know what I am doing."

And the odd thing of it was she *did* trust him, Penelope reflected a few minutes later, following the housekeeper up the stairs to her rooms. He was maddening, impossibly overbearing at times, and she knew next to nothing about him, and yet she trusted him. She didn't know if that made her a saint or a fool, and she prayed to heaven she would never find out which she was.

The following morning Daniel was up and gone from the house at the unfashionable hour of eleven o'clock. His first stop was his bank, where he made certain his bank draft from America had arrived. He also stopped at his solicitor's office, and was relieved when the older man accepted his change of identity with only nominal objections.

"I understand your position, Mr. Warfield," he said, regarding Daniel over the rims of his spectacles. "As a disgraced son it is probably best that you not use your given name, but I cannot help but wonder if you are doing the correct thing in posing as a *real* person."

"It is as I have explained, Mr. Landon," Daniel said, feeling a twinge of guilt at the lies and half-truths he'd been spinning since taking his seat. "I am only doing so to accommodate a neighbor. Mr. Grantham suffers from a condition which makes his appearing in public impossible, and he begged that I do this for him. Since I could not use my true name, I thought it would do no harm."

"No harm, perhaps, but you are risking scandal should your deception be discovered," Mr. Landon reproved with a shake of his head. "You could even be prosecuted, should the Royal Society chose to lay charges against you."

"Then we had best take care they never learn the truth," Daniel said smoothly, getting to the reason for his visit. "My man of business in America tells me you are member of the Royal Institution as well as several other scientific societies. Is that true?"

Mr. Landon removed his spectacles and began polishing them nervously. "Yes, I am," he admitted, "but I fail to see how that may be of any help to you."

"Because I wish you to see that I am properly introduced to the other members of these organizations," Daniel said, leaning forward to pierce him with a measuring glare. "The sooner people meet me as Ulysses Grantham, the sooner I will be accepted as Ulysses Grantham. Do you not agree?''

"I—I suppose that is so," Mr. Landon stammered, replacing his spectacles on his nose and dabbing at his forehead with his handkerchief. "But I can not approve of deceiving my friends. It is most unseemly."

"Perhaps," Daniel agreed, although his expression did not soften. "But you will do as I ask, won't you?"

"But what of Mr. Grantham's reputation?" Mr. Landon wailed, clearly not convinced. "I have heard of his work, and it sounds most dreadfully intricate. If you should make an error—"

"I won't make an error," Daniel interjected, recalling the voluminous notes Penelope had given him during the journey from Bibury. "Mr. Grantham has given me personal instruction in his theories and experiments, and his sister will be there to assist me should I falter."

"His sister?" Mr. Landon's nose twitched in disapproval.

"She is his assistant, and knows as much about his work as he does," Daniel replied coldly, not caring for the censorious note in the older man's voice. He'd decided to include his solicitor in the plot after a great deal of thought, knowing it would be impossible to keep the matter a secret from him. He was the only person in London aware of Daniel's true identity, and he wanted the man firmly on his side from the start.

"It still sounds a dangerous game to me," Mr. Landon opined with a sigh. "However, I suppose that is neither here nor there. As your solicitor it is my duty to protect you, and you may rely upon me to render whatever assistance you require."

"Good." Daniel allowed himself a moment to savor his victory before rising to his feet. "I will leave my address with your clerk; please direct any correspondence to me there as Mr. Ulysses Grantham."

"As you wish, Mr. Grantham," Mr. Landon agreed, regarding him solemnly. "But I should like to remind you that lies are rather like a bog. They are easy enough to stumble into, and almost impossible to get out of once you are caught. I trust you will remember that."

The solicitor's words were much on Daniel's mind as he returned to the house. He prided himself on his honor and his integrity, and it bothered him that he was compromising both with his actions. Unfortunately he could think of no other course to follow, and his mood was somber when he walked into the breakfast room and found Penelope and her mama engaged in a heated debate.

"It is pointless to argue, Mama, for my mind is set," Penelope said, her chin coming up in a fashion Daniel was beginning to recognize. "I refuse to rig myself out in sprigged muslin like a simpering deb simply because fashion declares it so! People must take me as I am or leave me be; I care not which."

"But Penelope, you must have a new wardrobe!" Mrs. Grantham insisted, her own chin coming up as well. "It was one thing for you to go about Bibury in those dreadful gowns of yours, but it is quite another in London!" She was about to add more when she saw Daniel standing by the door and immediately appealed to him.

"Oh Ulysses, thank heaven you are come!" she exclaimed, her eyes filling with tears. "Tell this unnatural sister of yours that she is being foolish beyond permission! Only look what she means to wear on our first tour of the city!"

The ease with which Mrs. Grantham fell into the role of his mama removed the last of Daniel's troublesome thoughts, and he dutifully turned his head to study Penelope.

She was wearing a simple gown of pale blue sarcenet, her slender shoulders covered by a fringed blue-and-rose-colored shawl. Her dark blond hair was in its customary chignon, and a few tendrils escaped confinement to curl about her ears and forehead. His first thought was that she looked perfectly enchanting. But with Mrs. Grantham's admonishments in mind he studied her more carefully, comparing Penelope's simple attire with the elegant clothing he had seen worn by the few fashionable ladies abroad at so early an hour.

"I fear mother is right," he said after a long moment. "Your dress is lovely, but it simply will not do."

As he expected, her eyes narrowed in fury. "And since when have you been an arbiter of fashion . . . *Ulysses*? I thought you too intellectual to concern yourself such frivolous matters.''

Daniel hid a grin at her truculent manner. ''An intelligent man concerns himself with a variety of interests,'' he drawled, aware of Carlyle standing behind him. He knew Penelope too well to think the butler's presence would prove an adequate deterrent, and he spoke quickly before her temper gave them all away. ''But even if I were as ignorant as a savage about such things, I would have but to look about me to know your gown is *outré*. Carlyle?'' He glanced over his shoulder.

''Yes, Mr. Grantham?'' The butler stepped forward, a bushy eyebrow lifting in haughty inquiry.

''Please arrange for my sister to be brought up to fashion,'' he said, enjoying himself to the hilt.

Carlyle didn't so much as blink. ''As you wish, Mr. Grantham,'' he said, executing a low bow. ''And shall I arrange the same for you? I am afraid your jacket is . . .'' His beak-like nose twitched in disapproval. ''Inappropriate,'' he concluded loftily.

Daniel glanced down, but before he could defend the offending garment, Penelope spoke. ''What an excellent suggestion!'' she exclaimed, beaming her approval at Carlyle. ''We wouldn't wish your employer to be taken for a quizz, would we?''

''No, Miss Grantham, we would not,'' the butler agreed gravely.

''In fact,'' she added, sliding Daniel a triumphant smirk, ''such a prospect would be quite lowering for a man in your position, wouldn't it?''

Daniel set down his fork with a thump. ''Why, you obnoxious— ''

''Ulysses, Penelope,'' Mrs. Grantham interrupted sternly, ''stop wrangling, and finish your meal! Your conduct is most unseemly.''

Daniel's cheeks warmed with embarrassment. ''She started it,'' he grumbled, picking up his fork with a sulky scowl.

''And I am putting an end to it,'' Mrs. Grantham returned, shaking her head in maternal disgust. ''Children!''

* * *

"I wish you'd stop laughing," Daniel complained, helping Penelope into the carriage. "It's not that funny."

"I shouldn't be so certain of that," she replied, her eyes sparkling with laughter at the mutinous expression on his face. "I daresay it's been a long time since your mama last read you such a thundering scold!"

To her dismay, a hard look stole over his face. "A long time, indeed," he agreed, and turned his head to gaze out the window, effectively ending the conversation.

Penelope bit her lip, realizing she had upset him. Again it occurred to her how very little she knew of him, and this time she decided to put a end to her ignorance.

"Tell me about America," she commanded with a bright smile, settling back against the padded leather seat. "Is it as wild and uncivilized a place as they say it is?"

He turned to her, his face still a cold mask. "Parts of it are," he agreed coolly. "Other parts are quite beautiful."

"What of where you live . . . Charleston, is it not?" she pressed, determined not to be put off.

The ice in his eyes faded as he considered her question. "Charleston is especially beautiful," he said after a moment. "State Street has as many fine homes as you could imagine, and the gardens have to be seen to be believed. When I first arrived in the city, the gardens were what enchanted me most."

Penelope had no interest in flowers, and waved his description aside. "What of scientific societies?" she asked, leaning forward to study him. "Are there many of them?"

A genuine smile softened his lips. "Several, as a matter of fact. Charleston is a port city, and trade is very important to the economy. Science, with the advances it brings, is of great interest to us all."

His prosaic reply diverted her attention. "Why should men in commerce be interested in such things?"

"Because it makes for better profits," he said, his eyes dancing. "Haven't you heard we Americans care for nothing else?"

Penelope smiled at the teasing words, and because he was being so forthcoming, she decided to press for even more.

"What of your father?" she asked curiously. "Is he in trade?"

The hard look returned to his face. "My father is dead," he said, his voice flat. "And he was a . . . farmer, I suppose you would call him. He left a good-sized estate to my brother."

She instantly regretted her impetuous question. "I am sorry," she said, laying her hand on his arm. "I lost my father almost two years ago, and I miss him still." She hesitated, then plowed ahead. "Is your mother alive?" she asked, not wishing to make another error.

He shook his head. "She died a few months before father did."

Penelope bit her lip, and silently called herself seven kinds of a fool. Another apology seemed inadequate, so she decided the safest course would be to change the subject.

"Have you had time to study the notes I gave you?" she asked, withdrawing her hand and leaning back in her seat. "I should be happy to answer any questions, should you have them."

He hesitated briefly before responding. "Actually, the notes you gave me are self-explanatory. There are a few things I still find puzzling, but we can discuss them later."

She frowned in concern. "Why can't we discuss them now?" she demanded, her brows pleating with worry. They hadn't discussed when they would be contacting the Royal Society, but she assumed it would be soon. He couldn't want to continue the charade indefinitely, she worried.

"Because there's something else we need to discuss first."

His evasive reply did little to calm her exacerbated nerves. "What is it?" she demanded, suspiciously.

His lips curved in a wry smile. "How very distrustful you sound," he drawled, folding his arms across his chest and regarding her with obvious amusement.

"Mayhap it is because I dislike the way you sidestep a direct question," she retorted, refusing to give way. "There are times, sir, when you are devilishly evasive."

His eyes narrowed and he sat forward. "Mayhap, madam, I simply prefer my privacy," he snapped. "But if it will calm you, I wish to discuss your role in our little game."

"My role?" her brows knitted in a scowl. "I thought it was already decided I would be your assistant."

"When we are in front of the Royal Society, yes, but I am talking about when we are out in public, as we are now."

"I thought that was also agreed," she said, recalling with resentment the pledge he had wrung from her. "I am to be your ever-obedient sister, demurely following your every command."

To her annoyance, he threw back his head and gave a roar of laughter. "Penelope, my sweet, I would have to be the biggest fool to ever draw breath were I to expect such a thing of you," he said, his deep voice rich with amusement.

Her cheeks grew warm, as much from the unexpected endearment as from his open pleasure. "Then it's just as well you're not a fool," she muttered, slumping lower against the cushions. "I never had the slightest intention of following your commands in the first place."

"I know," he said, his green eyes dancing. "But fortunately I am not interested in blind obedience from you. Although your willing cooperation would make for a pleasant change, especially once the Season starts."

"The Season?" She jerked her head back in astonishment. "What has the Season to do with us?"

"A great deal, actually," he replied after a thoughtful pause. "I've been thinking, and I've decided Ulysses would be better served by our partaking fully in the social round."

"But—"

"Think about it," he said, his expression solemn. "At the moment you are completely at the mercy of the Royal Society, subject to their every whim—and you may be very sure they are aware of that fact. However, if you were to have more than one patron, you would be far more independent . . . wouldn't you?"

Penelope remained silent as she considered his suggestion. She had to admit the thought of such independence was sweetly tempting, and a second patron would mean she could afford more equipment without asking her mama for funds. "But how should our attending a lot of tiresome balls help me obtain a patron?" she asked curiously. "The *ton* doesn't care for such matters."

"The *ton* may care more than you realize. Beneath their silk clothes and cravats they're as pragmatic as the next fellow, and no less unwilling to invest in a promising young scientist. Mr. Davy of the Royal Institution enjoys such patronage. Why shouldn't Ulysses do the same?"

Put that way, Penelope could see no logical reason why she should cavil. Still . . . "Would I have to attend many parties?"

"More than you should like, but not as many as you fear," he answered cryptically. "If it will ease your mind, I've already selected the man whose favor I am most interested in currying."

"Who?"

"Lord Haworth."

The name meant nothing to Penelope, but as she wasn't well-acquainted with the aristocracy, she didn't dwell on the matter. "I'm not sure," she said after a few moments. "It seems to me the more people you . . . Ulysses meets, the greater the risk of everything falling apart. My plan was for Ulysses to make his bows to the Royal Society and then return to the country. You are supposed to be a recluse, you know," she added, sending him a fulminating glare.

He smiled slightly. "I've managed to screw my courage to the sticking point," he drawled, and then surprised her by once more taking her hand. "I have already agreed to help you, and you in turn have agreed to follow my lead. All I am asking is that you keep your word. Is that so hard to understand?"

She met his earnest gaze, and then gave a heavy sigh. "I hate it when you take that reasonable tone with me," she grumbled. "It makes arguing with you quite impossible."

His smile widened. "Then you'll do as I ask?"

Since she knew he was only doing what he thought best, Penelope found it easy to surrender. "If I must," she said grudgingly, "and if I can attend whatever lectures and demonstrations I wish to."

He raised her hand to his lips for a brief kiss. "So long as such events don't coincide with important social functions, you may attend whatever lectures you please," he promised softly. "Thank you, Penelope. You shan't regret this, I promise you."

5

T he next week passed in a flurry of activity for Daniel. In between seeing to his and his new family's wardrobes, he set out to learn all that he could of Lord Haworth. He'd even toyed with the idea of engaging the services of a Runner, but in the end he decided it wasn't worth the risk. If Haworth did have anything to do with Richard's and James's deaths, he wasn't about to leave the marquess's fate to the vagaries of the law. If vengeance was required, he intended taking it himself.

He also took steps to establish himself socially, paying an exorbitant bribe to have his name placed on the books at Brooks and White's. He even signed on at Mabtons and Gentleman Jackson's Salon, knowing it would be easier to strike up a conversation in such convivial surroundings. His first day at Jackson's he encountered two men who had been in his forum at Oxford, but both men brushed past him without so much as blinking their eyes. Daniel didn't know whether to be relieved or insulted by their utter lack of recognition.

In addition to these strenuous duties he also took his new-found family about the city, delighting especially in Penelope's reaction to their exalted surroundings.

"So that is the famous Tower," she said, gazing up at the gray and white fortress overlooking the Thames. "I must say

I am disappointed. It looks rather an ordinary place to have enjoyed such a bloody history.''

"I am not sure enjoyed is the proper word in this instance," Daniel commented, smiling at the acerbic remark. "I should think endured would have been closer to the mark."

"The only thing one must *endure* is boredom," Penelope returned, turning her slender shoulder on the Tower. "And from what I have heard, boredom is not a term one would use in connection with the Tudors and their successors."

"Not unless one wished a closer view of the Tower than may have been comfortable," he agreed laconically. He was about to suggest they stop for tea when Mrs. Grantham grabbed his arm.

"Ulysses, do you know that gentleman?"

He froze at her words. "What gentleman?" he asked, his gaze sweeping the cobblestoned courtyard for a familiar face.

"Over there." Mrs. Grantham gave a discreet nod. "He is standing beside that obvious creature in the appalling bonnet. He's been watching you for several minutes now."

Daniel spotted the cyprian first—a youthful woman with overly blond hair and a painted face who was clinging shamelessly to the arm of a tall man with dark brown hair and eyes the color of peridot. His heart clenched as he studied the other man's features. The man had barely been out of leading strings the last time he had clapped eyes on him, but Daniel had no difficulty recognizing his youngest brother. *Andrew*!

"Don't stare!" Mrs. Grantham squeaked, giving Daniel's arm an admonishing squeeze. "He will see you."

"It is too late," Penelope said, unfurling her parasol and moving closer to Daniel. "He is coming this way."

"Well, at least he knows we are ladies," Mrs. Grantham grumbled in relief. "You can see he has left his friend to fend for herself. I should have been sunk with shame had he attempted to introduce us to her."

Daniel didn't answer; he couldn't have spoken had his life depended on it. Andrew was the very image of Richard at the same age, and seeing him was like seeing Richard once again. He was still struggling for control when Andrew joined them.

"Good afternoon, ladies, sir," he said coolly, his gaze resting on Daniel's face as he swept his hat from his head. "I apologize for disturbing you, but I was wondering if we have met. I am Burlington."

"My lord," Daniel found his voice with great difficulty. It was hard to speak, when all he wanted to do was gather his remaining brother to his breast and hold him fast. "I am Ulysses Grantham, and this is my mother, Mrs. Grantham, and my sister, Miss Penelope Grantham. We are your neighbors in Bibury."

The suspicious look faded from Andrew's face. "Perhaps that is why you look so familiar," he said, studying Penelope and her mother before returning his gaze to Daniel. "Can you tell me where and how we met? I am ashamed to admit I can not remember."

"Oh, we have never been formally introduced, Lord Burlington." Mrs. Grantham saved the day by giving a nervous giggle. "But doubtlessly you have seen us about the village. It is such a small place, is it not? Why, only yesterday Penelope was remarking how in Bibury she knew the name of every horse and dog within three miles of our house! Didn't you, love?"

Penelope picked up her cue without missing a beat. "A slight exaggeration on my part," she said, dropping him a curtsey. "I don't claim a friendship with every hound in the neighborhood, although I will own to a nodding acquaintance with most of the horses. Yours is a blood bay named Emir, if memory serves."

Andrew's brows lifted in obvious astonishment. "That's right," he exclaimed, his watchful attitude vanishing. "How did you know that?"

"My brother and I are rather fond of long walks, and we encountered your groom exercising Emir one day," she answered, her lips curving in an impish smile as she sent Daniel a smug look. "I thought him quite beautiful, but Ulysses was terrified of him."

"A blatant lie, my lord," Daniel defended himself quickly. "I was but lost in admiration of the steed."

"I see," Andrew said, his lips thinning in a manner that reminded Daniel of their mother. She used to get precisely that expression on her face when she was sniffing out one of his lies. "Perhaps I must have seen you one day, and that is why you seem so familiar."

"Perhaps." Daniel didn't know what else to say. He'd thought himself prepared to meet his brother, but the encounter was shredding his control. He wanted to escape, he wanted to stay, and the discord was tearing him apart.

"I have it!" Penelope gave Andrew a bright smile. "You must have attended one of my brother's lectures! Are you interested in science, my lord?"

Andrew looked confused once more. "I cannot say that I am," he said, frowning at Daniel. "Are you a scientist, sir?"

"Oh yes," Penelope spoke before Daniel could think of a reply. "He is far too modest to say so, but Ulysses is rather well-known. That is why we are in London. He is going to be giving a demonstration of his newest theory in front of The Royal Society of Scientific Inquiry. If you would care to attend, I am sure we could obtain a voucher for you. Couldn't we, Ulysses?" And she gave Daniel a discreet poke with her elbow.

"I should be honored," he managed, inclining his head politely. He could see Andrew's companion was growing restive, and saw that his brother was uncomfortably aware of the woman's displeasure. In another moment she would be stalking over to join them. Thinking quickly, he extracted one of the calling cards he'd had made, and offered it to Andrew with a low bow.

"Here is my card, sir. If you should decide you wish to attend, send me word and I will have a voucher waiting for you."

Andrew accepted the card silently. "Perhaps I shall do that," he said, tearing his gaze from Daniel's face long enough to send the irritated doxy a warning look. When he was satisfied she would make no trouble, he glanced back at Daniel.

"Thank you for your kindness, Mr. Grantham," he said, inclining his head with an odd formality. "It was a pleasure meeting you. Perhaps we shall meet again."

Daniel managed a polite nod. "Perhaps we shall," he

agreed quietly, wondering if he would survive a second encounter.

"Well, the cat has certainly been set amongst the pigeons now," Mrs. Grantham grumbled to Penelope the moment they were alone in the sitting room Daniel had set aside for their use. "His lordship thinks Mr. Canton is my son. However shall we explain Ulysses to him should they meet again?"

Penelope leaned back against the settee, her eyes closing in weariness as she rubbed her temples. "Don't fuss so, Mama," she said, wishing she was alone so that she could consider everything that had happened. "You are refining on nothing, I promise you."

"Nothing?" Mrs. Grantham's voice rose in indignation. "His lordship is a viscount! Only think of the mischief he could make for us should he pronounce Ulysses a fraud! We would be ruined."

"But Ulysses isn't a fraud," Penelope reminded her, opening her eyes and meeting her mother's worried gaze. "And even if he and Lord Burlington should meet, it is doubtful his lordship will note the difference. They spoke but a few moments; I'm sure he won't even recall what Ulysses looks like."

"Yes, that is so," her mother agreed, looking relieved. "And should his lordship say anything, we've but to pretend ignorance and he will have no choice but to let the subject drop. Still," she gave a frown, "it was rather odd, the way he kept staring at our Ulysses. It was almost as if he recognized him."

Penelope had also noted the marked way the viscount had studied Daniel, but she wasn't about to add to her mother's fretting by agreeing with her. "I should think that most unlikely," she said, rising to her feet and walking over to the fireplace. "Daniel said his connection to the Burlingtons was a tenuous one, and that he and the viscount had never met. Perhaps it is simply a matter of family resemblance," she added, hoping that would appease her mother.

"Perhaps." Her mother's dubious tone made it plain she was far from convinced. "Still, we shall have to keep our fingers crossed and pray they do not meet again. Things are complicated enough without our offending our most powerful neighbor.''

Penelope didn't answer, although she agreed with her mother's estimation of the situation. Things were indeed complicated, and she laid the blame for that directly at Daniel's feet. Cutting a dash in society was his idea, and if the vouchers for Almacks that had arrived in the morning's mail were any indication, things were about to become even more lively.

Her mother had burst into tears at the sight of the precious vouchers, but Penelope was reserving judgement. As she'd told Daniel, every person he met increased the potential for disaster, and despite her proud show of indifference, she really did care what others thought of her. She didn't relish the thought of her ruse being exposed in front of the *crème de la crème* of society, and she was beginning to have serious reservations about her plan and the man she had selected to help carry it out.

''Enough of his lordship.'' Her mama had evidently decided to accept her reassurances, and was on to a new topic. ''Tell me what you are going to wear to The Duchess of Croweville's ball tomorrow evening. One of your new gowns, I trust?''

Penelope shook off her dark thoughts and gave her mother an amused smile. ''Considering you had my other clothing sent back to Bibury, I should think that a safe assumption,'' she drawled, returning to sit beside her mother. ''And if it will relieve your mind, I had planned on wearing the rose silk.''

''The one with the ruffled hem?'' her mother asked with a frown.

''No, the one with the seed pearls.'' Penelope mentally shook her head at the thought of the extravagant wardrobe she now possessed. At Daniel's insistence she had gone to one of the finest modistes in London, and now owned a selection of gowns that would have made all but the wealthiest of debutantes weep with envy.

''An excellent choice,'' her mother said, nodding her head in approval. ''I have a lovely set of pearls my mama gave me when I married your father. You may wear them, if you like.''

Knowing her mama's suggestion was in truth a command,

Penelope murmured her agreement, and, if the truth were to be told, she was rather looking forward to wearing the gown. Daniel had been with her when she selected it, and he had commented she would look lovely in it. The realization that his opinion mattered made her start with horror, and she listened with only half an ear as her mother prattled on about all the balls and parties that were being planned.

Daniel joined them a quarter of an hour later just as the maid was bringing tea, and Penelope thought he looked unusually tired. His deep green eyes were filled with shadows, and his expression reminded her of the first day they had met. While her mother was busy pouring tea, she moved to sit beside him.

"Is everything all right?" she asked, studying his drawn face with a worried gaze. "You seem rather worn."

He glanced away, and she thought he was going to refuse to answer, but he finally met her gaze. "Everything's fine," he replied, laying a gentle hand on her arm. "I was just reviewing your notes on Volta's work, and my mind is in a whirl. Do you really comprehend all that nonsense about currents and charges?"

Penelope frowned slightly. From their previous conversations she knew he understood Volta's work almost as much as she did, and she wondered why he was being so evasive. "It's not nonsense once you understand the basic concepts uniting electricity and magnetism," she said, dismissing the puzzle with a mental shrug. "If you're interested in learning more, Sir Humphry Davy is giving a lecture on magnetism tomorrow afternoon at the Royal Institution. Perhaps you would care to attend?"

He accepted the cup of tea Mrs. Grantham had prepared before answering. "That might be a good idea," he said, his tone reflective as he took a thirsty sip. "I also think we should pay a visit to the Royal Society while we're about it. It is past time they were making Ulysses's acquaintance, don't you agree?" He flashed Penelope a roguish grin.

Even though she knew he was teasing her, Penelope took his question seriously. "Do you think that wise?" she asked, chewing her bottom lip. "They might insist you give a demonstration, and there is still a great deal I need to teach you."

"Let them insist," he said, dismissing the Society with a negligent shrug. "According to their own terms, I am to appear at their next public lecture, and that won't be held for several weeks. If they try pressing the matter, I will simply tell them to keep their cursed stipend and be done with them."

Penelope choked on the mouthful of tea she had just taken. "You will what?" she gasped, setting down her cup with a noisy clatter. "Have you lost your reason? You can not mean to do such a thing!"

"Certainly I can, if they think they can make me perform like a trained bear," he returned coolly, his lips thinning in anger. "I have been thinking, and I've decided that this Royal Society you go in such fear of needs you more than you need them. If they get too high-handed, tell them to go to the devil."

The retort Penelope was about to utter withered on her lips at this amazing observation. "What do you mean?"

His lips twisted in a half-smile. "I'm probably slitting my own throat by telling you this, but your work—that is, Ulysses's work—has generated a great deal of excitement in certain quarters. Since we've been in London, I've been invited to join no less than three scientific societies, all of which have made it plain that they would be delighted to sponsor a promising young scientist like Ulysses Grantham."

His words were music to Penelope's ears. "Really?" she asked, and then frowned in sudden annoyance. "Why didn't you tell me?"

His green eyes sparkled with silent laughter. "I believe I just did," he drawled. "What time will Mr. Davy be speaking?"

Penelope paused, not at all certain she wished to attend anything with so vexing a creature. But in the end the prospect of listening to the foremost scientists in England overcame her pique, and she surrendered with a resigned sigh. "Four o'clock," she said, folding her arms and sending him a challenging glare. "And he is *Sir* Humphry now; he was recently Knighted."

Sir Humphry then," he said, turning to her mother, who

was watching them with an indulgent smile. "Will you be joining us, Mother?" he queried, his manner smoothly solicitous.

"Heavens, no!" she exclaimed with a tinkling laugh. "I shouldn't understand a quarter of what was being said, and I fear I should find the whole thing quite boring. But certainly the two of you may go, if that is your wish. Only mind that you don't become overly tired," she said, wagging her finger at them. "I want you to be well-rested for tomorrow evening."

"Mama! As if attending a lecture could be so arduous!" Penelope replied, shaking her head at her mother's nonsense.

"Nonetheless, I want you to promise me you shall lie down the minute you return home," Mrs. Grantham said, ignoring Penelope's outburst. "I am sure your brother will agree that it simply won't do for you to appear at your first ball looking all wan and dragged-out. Isn't that so, Ulysses?" She turned to her counterfeit son for support.

To Penelope's fury, he didn't disappoint her. "You are quite right, Mama," he said, studying Penelope as if she were an exhibit in a menagerie. "We wouldn't want the *ton* to think she was possessed of a delicate constitution. Although I suppose it wouldn't go too amiss if she were to swoon now and again," he added, his smile deliberately taunting.

"I believe you have forgotten who is the invalid in this family, brother dearest," she said, her tone falsely sweet as she rose to her feet. "Now if you will excuse me, I believe I shall retire to my rooms. I feel a fit of the vapors coming on." She turned and stalked out, her chin raised high in defiance.

Daniel was still chuckling at the memory of her recalcitrant expression as he waited in the hall for Penelope to join him the following afternoon. Her prickly demeanor delighted him as often as it annoyed him, but he found it hard to remain angry with her overly long. Perhaps it was because he prefered her acerbic comments over the silly simpering and giggling of most ladies, he mused, recalling with a wince the chits he met his first season in London.

He also recalled how terrified he'd been in those first gut-wrenching weeks, when he'd felt like the biggest dolt to ever draw breath. Naturally being as filled with himself as only a nineteen-year-old boy could be, he'd refused to admit his fear, and had behaved as outrageously as possible. He fell in with a wild bunch of Corinthians, and would likely have tumbled headlong into the scandal broth had it not been for Richard.

His eldest brother had separated him from his loose-living companions by some mysterious means he'd never fully explained, and had taken him firmly in hand. Daniel had resented Richard's interference at the time, and it was only years later that he came to appreciate what Richard had done for him. He still shuddered to think what might have become of him had it not been for his brother's intervention.

"Well, I am ready; let us be off." The disgruntled voice came from just above his head, and he turned to see Penelope making her way down the winding staircase.

She was wearing one of her new gowns in rose and cream-striped silk, topped with a velvet spencer of darker rose. A matching silk parasol and a fetching bonnet in cream chipstraw completed the ensemble, and he thought she looked enchanting.

"It was well worth the wait," he said, moving forward to greet her. "You look perfectly lovely, Penelope."

"Perfectly ridiculous, you mean," she grumbled, making a face as she pulled on her gloves. "Mama made me wear it. She said it was what all the fashionably dressed young ladies are wearing, but *I* think it makes me look like a brainless chit."

Aware of the hovering footman, Daniel hastily revised the heartfelt compliment he had been about to pay her. "A brainless chit and a fashionably dressed young lady are usually one and the same thing," he drawled mockingly. "Now stop fussing over your appearance. We shall be late if you keep dawdling."

His words brought her finely arched eyebrows snapping together. "I wasn't fussing!" she denied, her hazel eyes snapping with outrage. "And I never dawdle."

"As you say," he said, affecting an older brother's exasperation. "Now, might we be on our way? As it is such an uncommonly lovely day, I thought we might walk. The

Royal Institution is less than a mile away, and I thought you might enjoy seeing something of the city.''

To his relief his suggestion found favor with her, and a few minutes later they were strolling down Mount Street toward the elegant homes lining Berkeley Square. They had walked less than four blocks when Penelope began to chuckle softly.

''What is it you find so amusing?'' he asked, taking her elbow as they scurried across the busy street.

''I was thinking it is a pity you aren't an actor,'' she admitted, once they were safely across. ''You play the part of an older brother to perfection. I vow, you're almost as aggravating as Ulysses can be when he puts his mind to the task.''

Her observation brought an answering chuckle to his lips, and he gave her a mocking grin. ''A workman is always worthy of his hire, Miss Grantham, but I am pleased if my humble efforts have found favor with you,'' he said piously, relieved she had recovered from her earlier fit of pique. It was one of the things he most liked about her. She might have the devil's own temper, but she seldom remained in the boughs very long.

''What rot, as if you have ever given a fig for my thoughts!'' she retorted, tossing her head back with a musical laugh. ''You are almost as arrogant as you are odious, but I have decided it is all part of your charm.''

He inclined his head with grave courtesy, accepting her teasing insult in the light-hearted spirit with which it was offered. ''Thank you, sister, you are too kind to me.''

''Not at all,'' she murmured, the laughter in her eyes growing more prounounced. ''And since I am pouring the butter over you, allow me to compliment you on your *toilet*. You look every inch the proper gentleman in those togs.''

To Daniel's amazement, he felt his cheeks grow warm. Although he was by no means a vain man, he'd taken considerable pains with his wardrobe that morning, and he couldn't help but be pleased by her words of praise. ''Once again, you are being too kind,'' he said, doing his best not to preen. ''But to be honest, the credit for my appearance is not truly mine. The valet Carlyle hired to serve me is a despot in a waistcoat, and any compliments you have ought best be paid to him.''

"Stuff, you look the very plate of fashion," she said, waving aside his attempts at modesty. "I daresay that when you make your bows tonight, you shall have all the giggling debs flocking to your side. They're already whispering about you," she added, sending him a smile too sweetly innocent to be genuine.

He jerked to a halt, genuinely appalled. "What?"

She laughed again. "Stop looking so horrified," she admonished, giving his arm a playful slap. "It's not as if they're going to take to swooning around you, like they do Byron. At least," she paused thoughtfully, "I do not think they will."

Her words unleashed some of the tension coiling in him, and he gave her a suspicious scowl. "Are you twigging me?" he demanded, praying such was the case. It would prove disastrous to his plans if he were to draw undue attention to himself, and he had worked too hard to risk losing everything now.

"Perhaps," she drawled, eyes gleaming with amusement. "And perhaps I am merely getting a little of my own back. Something you would do well to remember the next time you take it into your head to accuse me of dawdling."

He stared at her for several seconds and then began chuckling. "No wonder your brother made himself a recluse," he said, the warm amusement in his voice removing any sting his words might have contained. "You would drive a saint to exasperation with your conniving ways."

"Perhaps," she repeated, her gaze meeting his in deliberate challenge. "But you are rather too full of yourself to compare yourself to a saint. You're hardly a holy man, sir."

Daniel felt his smile fade. He knew she was teasing, but that didn't lessen the flash of pain ripping through him. He hastily assumed a cool expression before glancing away.

"No, but I will be a late one, if we do not hurry," he said, lengthening his stride as they turned down Grafton Street. "According to *The Post*, Sir Humphry's lectures begin sharply on the hour, and if we aren't there early we won't have a chance at being admitted. Hurry now." He kept walking, ignoring her indignant gasps to slow down.

* * *

Why the devil did I say that? Penelope wondered glumly, listening with only half an ear as Sir Davy explained a function of magnetism she already understood. She and Daniel had managed to get a seat close to the front of the lecture hall, and she had an unobstructed view of the great scientist and the experiment he was presenting. Under any other circumstances such good fortune would have her dancing a jig, but at the moment she was too heartsick.

She stole a furtive glance at Daniel, noting that although he was gazing at the stage, he seemed as distracted and somber as she felt. She was coming to know him, and she knew that when his eyes got that dark, distant look, it meant he was lost in thoughts he never shared with her.

The realization was oddly hurtful, and she glanced quickly back at Sir Humphry. What thoughts could Daniel have to cause him such sorrow? she wondered bleakly. Despite numerous attempts, she still knew little of his life in America and why he had elected to return to England. She had tried asking but he'd rebuffed her continually, and as she'd feared offending him, she'd allowed the matter to drop. Now she wondered if that had been a mistake. Clearly there had to be some reason why such a handsome, intelligent man as Daniel should be so secretive.

Handsome. She shifted uneasily, her cheeks flushing with color. As an intellectual, she considered herself above mooning over men, and yet she couldn't deny that Daniel attracted her more than was proper. She glanced at him again, thinking how dashing he looked in his jacket of dark blue superfine, his starched cravat tied in an elegant arrangement about his throat. Every other man in the large auditorium was dressed in a similar fashion, yet they all paled when she compared them to Daniel.

Perhaps it was his intelligence that made him seem different, she brooded, or the proud way he carried himself. He might be an American, but there were times when he seemed as highborn as an English lord, and certainly he had more of a sense of honor than any lord she'd ever had the misfortune of meeting.

An image of Lord Burlington flashed in her mind, and she

frowned as a sudden cognizance struck her. Daniel had always claimed his relation to the Burlingtons was a distant one, but now that she thought of it, he and Lord Burlington looked close enough in appearance to be brothers. Oh, Daniel was taller and more muscular than the viscount, but there was something in the way they both moved, in the shapes of their heads, that made her wonder if their association was closer than Daniel would admit.

The thought was intriguing, but before she could dwell on it further, Sir Davy began discussing the enticing properties of electricity. She leaned forward eagerly, determined to put the matter out of her mind. But even as part of her listened in rapt attention to the inspiring lecture, the other part was puzzling over Daniel and the mystery of who he was and who he was not. It was a puzzle she was determined to solve.

6

The ball was already in progress when Penelope and her family arrived at the Crowevilles' elegant house on Cavendish Square. Once they'd made their bows to the duke and duchess they followed the footman to the ballroom, where the strains of music could scarce be heard above the roar of conversation. The sight of so many people, all packed into so small a space, brought Penelope to an abrupt halt.

"Good heavens!" she exclaimed, her hand tightening on Daniel's arm as she gazed about her in undisguised horror. "Did the Crowevilles invite the whole of London to this thing?"

"It does seems as if they did," Daniel agreed quietly, his cool gaze sweeping over the crowded ballroom.

"Pooh," her mother sniffed, her plump body quivering with excitement. "It is nothing more than a fashionable squeeze. Why, I have heard it said that no party can be counted a success unless half the ladies present swoon from the heat and crowds."

"Then this ball shall certainly be considered a triumph for her grace," Penelope muttered, fanning herself vigorously. "I am already feeling as if I shall collapse, and we have only just arrived. However do the dancers endure it?"

"Because they must," Mrs. Grantham said, bending a frown on Penelope. "And remember what I said. You are not

69

to dance the waltz until you have been introduced at Almacks next Wednesday. No proper lady would dream of waltzing until the patronesses have given her the nod.''

"Yes, Mama,'' Penelope replied, thinking it was unlikely she would be asked to dance at all. At the few assemblies she attended in Bibury she'd been left standing in the corner like a piece of forgotten statuary, and she much doubted it would be any different here. Despite her new clothes and the pains she'd taken with her appearance she still felt the same inside, and her fragile confidence wavered.

As if sensing her disquiet, Daniel gave her hand a comforting squeeze. "I don't know how to waltz either,'' he confessed, his lips curving in a wry smile. "Shall I have Carlyle engage a dancing master so that we might remedy our appalling ignorance?''

"That might be best,'' she agreed, grateful he had mistaken the reason for her unhappiness. It would be beyond humiliating if he ever learned the truth.

"I will see to it at once,'' he promised, giving her hand another pat before turning his attention to the crowds. "Now, you must tell me how things are done here. Do we wait for people to approach us, or are we free to approach them? I fear I can not recall the exact procedure.''

"What do you mean you can not recall?'' Mrs. Grantham demanded, her brows knitting in a frown. "I thought you were unfamiliar with our society.''

Penelope saw Daniel stiffen, and jumped in to protect him. "I told you he spent a term at Oxford, Mama,'' she said, adapting the tone she used to let her mother know she considered her embarrassingly slow. "One may suppose he was invited to at least a few social functions during that time.''

"Very few,'' Daniel agreed quickly, his manner as unruffled as ever. "And it was a number of years ago.''

"Well, you might have said so without taking my head off, Penelope,'' Mrs. Grantham retorted, sending her an aggrieved scowl. "I merely asked him to clarify himself.''

"I apologize, Mother,'' Penelope said, lowering her eyes in mock penitence. "I didn't mean to snap at you. All the excitement has put me in a temper, I suppose.''

"Humph!" Her mother snorted, unfurling her fan with regal dignity. "We shall say no more of the matter now. But to answer your question, Ulysses, it is usually considered best to wait until one is approached before engaging others in conversation. We would not wish to be taken for cits."

"I shall bow to your superior knowledge, Mother," Daniel said, accompanying his words with a graceful movement of his head. "But in any case, I believe the matter is about to be taken out of our hands."

Penelope glanced up and saw a group of young people bearing down on them. A slender brunette with blue eyes was the first to speak, her smile friendly as she offered her hand to Penelope.

"Good evening," she said, her voice pleasantly cultured. "I pray you will not think me overly bold, but did I not see you at Sir Humphry's lecture this afternoon?"

"Yes, you did," Penelope answered, the knot of fear in her stomach uncoiling at the woman's words. "It was the first time I have had the pleasure of hearing him speak, and I must say I found it most interesting."

"As did I," the brunette assured her, her gaze flicking momentarily to Daniel before glancing back at Penelope. "I am Miss Lynette Chartfield, and this is my dear friend, Miss Georgina Reynolds. The handsome rogue with us is my cousin, Mr. Marcus Bellamy. He is only interested in antiquities, so he did not accompany us to the Institution."

"An obvious oversight on my part I shall take pains not to repeat," Mr. Bellamy said, his brown eyes sparkling with good humor as he executed a sweeping bow. "Had I any notion such a dusty subject as magnetism attracted so beauteous an audience, I should have been there *tout de suite*, I assure you."

Penelope blinked at him, amazed to realize he was flirting with her. Such an event was so far out of her realm of experience that she had no notion how to respond, and gaped at him in confusion. She was casting about in her mind for an acceptable reply when Daniel stepped forward to rescue her.

"I am Ulysses Grantham," he said smoothly, capturing Miss Chartfield's hand and carrying it to his lips. "Allow me to introduce you to my mother, Mrs. Grantham, and my sister, Miss Penelope Grantham. It is an honor to meet you and your friends, Miss Chartfield.''

"Mr. Ulysses Grantham?" Miss Reynolds repeated, brushing past Miss Chartfield to gaze up at Daniel with wide eyes. "Are you the Mr. Grantham who wrote the article "On The Principles of Water and Electricity" for *The Lady's Diary*?"

Penelope gave Daniel a discreet nudge, and was relieved when he took the hint at once. "I am," he said, giving Miss Reynolds a dazzling smile. "It is gratifying to know someone other than myself read it."

"Oh, but you must know everyone read it!" Miss Reynolds all but gushed, her gray-blue eyes earnest as she gazed up at Daniel. "After all, the editor asked you to write a second article expounding on your theory, did he not?"

"You must forgive my brother, Miss Reynolds," Penelope said quickly, sliding her hand into the crook of Daniel's arm and sending him a fond look. "I fear he is far too modest for his own good. It never occurs to him others might read his work."

"Oh, I have read all your articles," Miss Reynolds said, her cheeks flushing as she continued gazing up at Daniel. "I am looking forward to your presentation at The Royal Society. Are you going to be discussing Ampre's work with batteries? I think it very mean spirited of the Committee to dismiss his work merely because he is French. Do you not agree?"

The question sparked a lively debate that soon attracted the interest of others standing nearby, and in no time at all a small group had formed around them. Penelope was feeling quite flush with success when she felt the touch of a hand on her arm, and turned to find Miss Chartfield regarding her with a polite smile.

"Your brother is a most intelligent man, Miss Grantham," she commented, her blue eyes bright with curiosity as she studied Penelope. "You must be proud of him."

"He has his moments," Penelope agreed, watching indulgently while Daniel use his well-shaped hand to illustrate some point he was making.

"Yes, but I had heard he was an invalid who shunned the

company of others," Miss Chartfield pressed. "I am surprised to find him so convivial."

A frisson of alarm trailed down Penelope's spine. She had anticipated something of this sort and even had a full explanation prepared, but she hadn't expected to have his identity challenged quite so soon.

"Ulysses injured his spine in a fall from a horse, and he was very ill for a number of years," she said confidentially, repeating the woeful tale she had concocted. "The experience left him shy and somewhat wary of other people, and it is only recently that we've been able to convince him to join in the social round. I do hope you will be patient with him, ma'am," she added, her lips stretching in a thin smile. "Despite appearances he is still quite shy, and any criticism is likely to send him scurrying back to Bibury, never to emerge again."

Miss Chartfield stared at her for several seconds, and then broke into a soft chuckle. "What a dreadful cat you must think me!" she said, shaking her dark curls ruefully. "I meant no offense, I promise. It is only that I am surprised to find him so handsome and charming. He is certain to cut a dash amongst the ladies," she added in an obvious attempt at humor.

Penelope relaxed, relieved Miss Chartfield had accepted her story so easily. "Yes, so long as those ladies can converse on the subjects of electricity and magnetism," she said, affecting a light laugh. "I fear when it comes to more mundane topics, poor Ulysses becomes quite lost."

"Mmm." Miss Chartfield arched a dark eyebrow as a stunning blond in a gown that barely escaped indecency joined their group and began flirting outrageously with Daniel. "In that case, I am predicting those subjects are about to become imminently fashionable amongst the London ladies. Your brother seems to have taken."

Before Penelope could reply Mr. Bellamy approached them, and much to Penelope's amazement, asked her to stand up with him.

"Your mother has already told me you can not waltz," he said, sending her an audacious smile. "But she did say you might join me for a country dance, if you would like to, that is.''

Penelope brightened with pleasure. She wasn't such an antidote she had never been asked to dance, but this was one of the few times an attractive man had sought her out without prompting from well-meaning friends.

"I should like that very much," she said, not caring that she was behaving with less than sophisticated ennui. Suddenly she wanted to dance more than anything else, even if Mr. Bellamy wasn't the partner she would have secretly preferred.

Fortunately Mr. Bellamy was far too much of a gentleman to comment on her eagerness, and they joined the crowd lining up for the country dance. He proved an able and charming partner, and Penelope's cheeks were flushed with laughter and exertion when he escorted her back to the corner where her mama and the others were waiting.

"You are a most accomplished dancer, Miss Grantham," he said, smiling as he bent over her hand. "May I be so bold as to lay claim to a waltz when the patronesses grant you permission?"

"That would be lovely, sir," she replied happily, thinking this society business was far easier than she had feared. She had been dreading making a cake of herself, but so far the evening was turning out quite well.

This optimistic thought had scarce formed when she felt the touch of a hand on her shoulder, and turned to find Daniel standing beside her.

"I am not certain I wish Penelope to perform the waltz," he said, studying the other man coolly. "I do not consider it quite proper for an unmarried female."

Mr. Bellamy's boyish face suffused with embarrassment. "Certainly, Mr. Grantham," he said hastily, his brown eyes darting toward Penelope's mother. "I meant no offense, I assure you. Your mother had already given her permission and—"

"My mother is not the head of this family," Daniel interrupted, his manner polite but firm. "I am. I would prefer you seek my permission, before approaching my sister again. I am sure you understand."

"Oh yes, indeed," Mr. Bellamy replied, executing a hasty bow.

"Excellent." Daniel's lips moved in a slight smile. "Now if you will excuse us, I believe my sister would like a breath of fresh air. Come, Penelope," and he led her off before she could utter a word of protest.

He guided her across the room and out onto the stone terrace overlooking the Crowevilles' garden, taking care to close the French doors behind them. The moment they were alone Penelope whirled around to face him, fully prepared to do battle. "How dare you behave like an overbearing papa!" she raged, her eyes glittering in fury. "You had no right to talk to Mr. Bellamy like that!"

His green eyes were dancing as he met her gaze. "As your elder brother I have every right," he told her, his lips curving in a taunting smile. "And so long as the world thinks that is what I am, that is how I shall behave. If you wish to inform Mr. Bellamy I am not your brother, you are free to do so."

Penelope recognized a trap when she saw one, but she refused to surrender the field without a fight. "If you were truly Ulysses, you wouldn't have noticed had I danced a jig with Prinny himself," she informed him grumpily, folding her arms beneath her breasts and turning away.

"Perhaps." He laid a gentle hand on her shoulder, and turned her around to face him. "But then, I'm not really Ulysses, am I?"

Penelope glanced up, her heart racing as their eyes met. For a moment she wasn't certain what emotions she saw reflected in the emerald depths of his eyes, and her own senses whirled in sweet confusion. It also occurred to her he had been having a bit of fun at her expense, and she sought refuge in indignation.

"I suppose I shouldn't be so surprised," she grumbled. "You warned me you would be an ogre, and it seems you have kept your word."

There was a short pause, then she heard a soft chuckle. "I believe I said I would be firm," he corrected, his tone wry. "That is hardly the same thing."

She swung back to face him, pride demanding she match

his light mood. "I disagree, sir," she retorted, raising her chin with a sniff. "With you, they are one and the same thing. Now, let us rejoin the others. I refuse to spend my first ball being brought to task by my domineering elder brother."

Daniel spent the rest of the evening surrounded by a circle of gushing young ladies. He was vain enough to find their attentions flattering, even as part of him winced at the interest they were drawing with their incessant giggling and sighing. He hadn't felt so much on display since attending his first ball in Charleston, where his accent and ties to the aristocracy had made him a highly sought *parti*.

Remembering his first weeks in America brought back a flood of bittersweet memories. He'd travelled to Charleston determined to make a life for himself far away from the stultifying influence of his family, and yet it had been his family's name and prestige that contributed most to his early success. The merchants of Charleston liked the notion of having the son of a viscount arranging their trade, and certainly his knowledge of the tastes of the upperclass had helped as well. But it was his connections to the *ton* that had proven his greatest asset. Even now, all these years later, he wasn't certain how he felt about that.

"Good evening, Mr. Grantham. How pleasant to see you again."

The quiet voice, edged with reserve, brought Daniel snapping back to the present, and he found himself face to face with his brother. After absorbing the shock, he gave Andrew a low bow.

"Good evening, my lord," he said, forcing himself to relax. "I am honored that you remember me."

Andrew's green eyes hardened imperceptibly. "I have been told I have a prodigious memory for names," he said, meeting Daniel's gaze in unmistakable challenge. "I possess an equal memory for faces, and yours is quite familiar. I am certain we've met before, and it was not at a lecture. Eventually I shall remember the where and when of it. When I do, we shall talk."

Daniel raised an eyebrow, acknowledging the underlying

threat with a cool smile. "Perhaps," he agreed in a mocking drawl.

Andrew studied him a long moment. "Good night, Mr. Grantham," he said, and turned and walked away without another word.

"I was unaware you were acquainted with his lordship," Miss Chartfield observed, fanning herself idly as she watched the viscount disappear into another room.

"He's our nearest neighbor in Bibury," Daniel replied, wondering how much she had heard and what she thought about it. Unlike the other ladies clustered about him she was genuinely interested in his supposed work, and the sharp gleam in her eyes warned him she was every bit as sharp as Penelope. A terrifying possibility when one thought of it, he mused, glancing around him until he found Penelope. She was standing across the room in earnest conversation with a young man with wavy blond hair.

"That would explain it," Miss Chartfield said, snapping the plumed fan shut, her lips set in a stiff smile. "Lord Burlington has never expressed an interest in science or indeed in any intellectual pursuit, to the best of my knowledge. His interests are said to lie in . . . other directions."

Daniel remembered the sly remarks the man at the inn had made about Andrew's ladybirds, and he was faintly shocked a well-bred lady like Miss Chartfield should be aware of such gossip. He also realized it meant she must know his brother, and he was eager to turn that to his advantage.

"Are you well-acquainted with the viscount, Miss Chartfield?" he asked, feigning polite interest as he smiled down at her.

She sniffed and angled her chin higher in a manner that was reminiscent of Penelope. "I am not," she said, her tone sharp. "But from what I have observed, his lordship is naught but a libertine and a wastrel; hardly the sort of man whose company I should care to cultivate."

"But you know him well enough to criticize him to other people, it would seem," Daniel said, and was then appalled by his lack of control. For a moment he feared he had revealed too much, but fortunately Miss Chartfield did not seem to notice.

"You are quite right, sir," she said quietly, her cheeks pinking with embarrassment. "I do not know his lordship at all well, and it was wrong of me to criticize him to others. Please forgive my indiscretion?" she added, lifting her head to meet his gaze head on.

"It is forgotten," Daniel assured her, relieved she had not taken offense. "Would you care to take a walk about the room with me?"

She accepted his arm, and a few moments later they were standing beside Penelope and the young man whom she introduced as Dr. Randolph Baker. Although the name was unfamiliar to him, it was obvious Miss Chartfield was better informed.

"Dr. Baker, it is an honor to meet you," she said, offering him her hand. "I had not heard you were in London."

"I arrived late yesterday, Miss Chartfield," he said, thrusting a hand through his tumbling golden locks. "The duke is a cousin of my mother's, and he has graciously invited me to stay with them. I shall be here for the Season."

"Dr. Baker is from Scotland, Ulysses," Penelope said, her hazel eyes flicking to Daniel's face. "He has some rather interesting gossip to share with us."

Her tense tone, as well as the fury he could see simmering in her eyes, warned Daniel something was afoot, and he steeled himself for what was to come. He turned to Dr. Baker, deciding he didn't care for the handsome, rather effeminate man.

"Indeed?" he asked, his voice pitched at its most intimidating level. "How intriguing. I was unaware scientists engaged in idle gossip."

Dr. Baker's face turned a bright shade of red. "It is not precisely gossip, Mr. Grantham," he said, his hand creeping up to tug at his cravat. "I was merely telling your sister that your latest research has sparked some lively debates in Edinburgh."

"They are saying you didn't originate your theory concerning the dual nature of electricity,'' Penelope said, making no attempt to disguise the outrage in her voice. "They've all but accused you of outright theft!"

Daniel hastily reviewed the voluminous notes Penelope had pressed upon him. "I never claimed to have originated it," he said, recalling a particular article on the subject. "I was but attempting to prove electricity, like magnetism, is possessed of both negative and positive qualities."

Dr. Baker looked more uncomfortable than ever. "Yes, well, as to that, a friend of mine, Edwyn Collister, conducted an experiment last year that resembles the work you are now claiming as your own," he mumbled, beginning to edge away from them. "He—he means to challenge your claim in front of the Royal Society."

"What?" The muted roar came from both Daniel and Miss Chartfield. "But that is absurd, Doctor!" she said, fixing the unfortunate man with an icy glare. "I've followed Mr. Grantham's work for almost two years, and it is most certainly his own. Your Mr. Collister is mistaken in his vile accusations."

"But Miss Chartfield, I assure you he—"

Daniel stepped forward, anxious to put an end to the conversation before Penelope made a scene. "I think it would be best if we leave this discussion for another time and place," he said. "In the meanwhile, Dr. Baker, might I suggest you refrain from repeating your friend's claims until he has proven them? There are legal steps one may take to protect oneself from malicious tattle, and do not think I won't stoop to employ them."

Dr. Baker paled so dramatically Daniel wondered if the man-millner was about to swoon. "You—you are threatening me with legal action?" he stammered, his voice quivering in horror.

"I am threatening nothing," Daniel answered, taking cold pleasure in the younger man's fear. "I am stating a fact. Slander me or my family, and the price you pay will be high indeed. Mark me on this, sir, for I am in dead earnest."

Dr. Baker wet his lips twice before managing to find his voice. "I—I mark you, Mr. Grantham," he said, swallowing nervously. "I mark you well."

* * *

"It will be easy, you said. You won't have to do anything, you said," Daniel muttered, pacing the confines of the library in scarcely controlled fury. "It is just as well I rejected your original offer, madam. The paltry twenty pounds you dangled in front of me would hardly have proven adequate compensation for all you have put me through this night!"

Penelope stirred restlessly, finding it difficult to remain silent beneath the lash of Daniel's tongue. She was willing to concede he had a right to be annoyed, but that didn't give him leave to ring a peal over her head. It was *her* name and work under attack, she reminded herself with a sniff; not his.

"Really, sir," she began, striving to remain calm, "I am hardly at fault if some miscreant has taken it into his head to claim my work as his own. I am just as dismayed as you are."

"Perhaps." He threw the concession to her with a grudging scowl. "But it's not you who shall have to defend yourself in front of the Royal Society, is it?"

She jerked in response to the tart observation. "I shall be there to help you," she muttered, her spirits sinking as she slumped lower on her chair. When she'd first conceived of having Daniel pose as Ulysses, it had never occurred to her a situation like this might arise. Now that it had, she was furious with herself for not anticipating it. A good scientist planned for every eventuality, and that she had failed to do so irritated her almost as much as Dr. Baker's accusations.

"It could have been worse, I suppose," Daniel said, pausing in front of the fire to loosen his cravat. "At least Baker had the good grace to warn us of Collister's accusations so we shall have time to prepare our defense." His gaze cut back to where she was sitting. "I trust his claims are without foundation?"

She was out of the chair and standing before him in a flash. "How dare you!" she exclaimed, her hands clenching in fury.

To her annoyance he merely laughed, cupping her shoulders in his hands and holding her easily in place. "Sheath your claws, little cat," he told her with a provocative smile. "I meant no insult, I promise you. I am merely attempting to discern where we stand that I might better defend our position."

His explanation did little to mollify Penelope's temper. "You call it no insult when you ask if this—this blackguard's charges are without foundation?" she demanded, her eyes snapping with the force of her emotions.

"A poor choice of words," he allowed, making no move to release her. "What I meant to ask is have you any idea why Collister should be making such a claim? Do you know him?"

Penelope paused before deciding to let his insult and the matter he was still holding her pass. "No," she admitted, shaking her head. "Nor is his name familiar to me, as is Dr. Baker's."

Daniel frowned slightly. "Why is his name familiar?"

"I recall reading several articles he wrote for one of the journals," she said, her own brows knitting as she struggled to remember the specifics. "They dealt for the most part with chemistry, as I recall, and they were very well written."

"Did any of them address electricity or magnetism?"

She thought some more. "No, I would have cut them out and set them aside if they had. And I am positive I never corresponded with either Mr. Collister or Dr. Baker," she added as the thought occurred to her. "Which is rather odd when you think about it."

"Why?"

"Well," she cleared her throat, not wishing to sound too full of herself. "I . . . rather, Ulysses, is considered something of an expert in the area, and I have exchanged letters with almost every scientist in England who has even a passing interest in the matter. If this Collister person is conducting experiments in electrical properties, he is doing so quite on his own."

"Hmmm." Penelope was released at last when Daniel dropped his hands and resumed his pacing. "Hmmm," he said again, his manner so enigmatic that Penelope quite lost her patience.

"Hmmm, what?" she asked, aware she sounded sharp as a shrew.

"Hmmm it has suddenly occurred to me to wonder if you are not the only one who posseses an alter ego," he said, draping his arm on the mantelpiece as he turned to study her.

The thought was so astounding that Penelope was momentarily knocked back apace. "What do you mean?"

"I mean," Daniel said slowly, "what if there is no Mr. Collister? What if the person making these outlandish claims is Dr. Baker himself?"

"But that is absurd!" Penelope gasped in disbelief. "Whatever could he hope to gain from such a pose?"

"Money, notoriety, perhaps even the stipend itself," he ticked off the possibilities with cool consideration. "You did mention the Society was cutting up stiff about it. How do you think they will respond to Mr. Collister's accusations?"

Penelope paled at the thought of yet another possibility she had failed to consider. "I do not know," she confessed, swallowing back her tears, "but I can not think they will be pleased. These societies are really no more than private clubs, you know, and they value their good reputation above all else."

Daniel remained silent, drumming his fingers on the mantle and staring off into space. "Miss Chartfield seemed to know the good doctor quite well, or at least, know of him. Perhaps I shall call on her tomorrow and pick her brain," he said at last.

Penelope felt her drooping spirits lift at the news. She had taken to the other woman at once, and rather fancied the thought of calling such an elegant and intelligent lady her friend. "Do you think I ought to go with you?" she asked, studying him hopefully. "It might look odd if you were to go alone."

"Not so odd as all that," he said, a knowing smile lifting his lips. "But you are more than welcome to join me, if you would like. In fact, it might be better if you do accompany me. You'll know better than I what sort of questions to ask her."

"Regarding Dr. Baker, do you mean?"

He nodded. "I especially want to know more about those articles he wrote, what societies he belongs to—that sort of thing. I'll ask around the clubs and see what sort of reputation he has there, if he has one.''

"I'm sure he does not; his cousin is a duke, after all," Penelope said, thinking the other man was too much a dandy to indulge in any riotous living.

To her surprise Daniel gave a derisive laugh. "Don't be a simpleton, Penelope," he said bitterly. "Having noble blood doesn't preclude one from being a villain. If anything, it makes such a thing even more likely.''

Given his own connections to the Burlingtons Penelope thought this a harsh assessment, but then she remembered he was not really English. "I'd forgotten you are an American," she commented with a teasing laugh. "Mind you take care to keep such sentiments to yourself. I would not wish it bandied about that Ulysses Grantham holds such shockingly egalitarian views.''

She'd meant her words as a jest, but if the odd look that stole over Daniel's face was any indication, she had fallen short of the mark.

"But I *am* an American, Miss Grantham," he said quietly, his expression surprisingly bleak. "Never forget that, because I promise you, I have no intention of doing so.''

7

This oblique comment was much on Penelope's mind when she rose the following morning. Having been in town long enough to acquire a touch of bronze, she took the precaution of sending Miss Chartfield a note asking permission to call upon her at her earliest convenience. After careful thought she also sent a note to Mr. Varney, the librarian at the Royal Society who had proven so helpful to her in the past. If Mr. Collister existed and was a member of the Society, she was certain he would know of it.

With those chores done she went down to the breakfast room to inform Daniel of her actions, only to find the wretch had already breakfasted and left for the morning.

"But where could he have gone?" she asked, pouting as she took her place at the table. "I thought we were going to spend the afternoon together."

"Really, Penelope, you mustn't be so selfish as to expect your brother to live in your pocket," her mother reproved, frowning at her over the rim of her coffee cup. "Ulysses is a grown man, and we must allow him his freedom. Besides, he did say he would be back in time for luncheon, so you are fretting over nothing."

"I wasn't fretting," Penelope defended herself with a disgruntled sigh. "I was but expressing concern that he had forgotten we'd spoken of calling upon Miss Chartfield."

"Oh?" Mrs. Grantham asked, looking pleased. "But that is wonderful! Is he sweet on her, do you think?"

Penelope took a sip of the rich coffee the footman had poured for her. "How am I to know?" she asked sourly, wondering why her parent's question annoyed her. "They met but last night."

"Yes, but he was rather singular in his attentions to her," her mother replied, her eyes gleaming with match-making fervor. "It would make a very credible match for them both, for she is said to be as taken with science as he is."

Penelope gaped at her, but with the footman and maid standing so close there was little she could say. The moment the servants withdrew, however, she leaned forward to study her mother's face.

"Mama, have you forgotten Mr. Canton isn't really Ulysses?" she asked gently. "He is an American, and he'll be returning to his home once all this nonsense is behind us."

Now it was her mother who stared. "Heavens, gel, what an astonishing question!" she said, setting her cup down with a clatter. "Of course I haven't forgotten! Never say you are jealous of the way I treat Mr. Canton?" she added, shooting her an accusing glance. "That is rather too bad of you, Penelope."

"I am not in the least jealous!" Penelope denied hotly, her face flaming with color. "I simply meant that when we are alone like this, there is no reason for you to keep up the subterfuge."

"No reason for you, mayhap," Mrs. Grantham huffed, "but I lack your innate gift of sophistry. I treat Mr. Canton as my son in private, because if I neglect to do so, I may forget to do it when we are in public."

That made such good sense Penelope felt like a perfect fool. Feeling perverse, she decided it was all Daniel's fault, and soothed her tender feelings plotting nebulous forms of revenge. Conversation became commonplace after that, as she and her mother passed the rest of the meal exchanging excited reminiscences about their first London ball.

The post arrived just as they were about to rise from the table, and a quick glance revealed nothing but a few invitations and the latest fashion journal. Watching her mama tearing into the invitations held little interest for Penelope, and she hastily excused herself.

"But don't you want to help?" her mother protested, glancing up from the note she had just opened. "There are several cards here that will require a personal response."

"I'll look at them later," Penelope promised, edging toward the door. "It is such a lovely day, I thought I might walk to the bookshop on Curzon Street and see if they have anything new."

"Do you think that wise?" her mother asked, looking worried. "We're not in Bibury any more, and I am quite sure Ulysses would not approve. He did say we were to observe all the proprieties, you know," she added, her tone reproachful.

This motherly observation brought Penelope's jaws clamping together. "I was unaware I was answerable to Ulysses for my every action," she said, her pride stirring with her temper.

Subtlety, as usual, was lost upon her mother. "Well, you are," she informed Penelope tartly. "And he has already said you are not to stir from this house alone. If you are so set to visit this bookshop then by all means do so, but you will take a footman or a maid with you."

Penelope knew this to be a reasonable request, but that didn't make accepting it any easier. Muttering a most unladylike sentiment beneath her breath, she turned and stalked out of the room, shouting for a maid in a hoydenish manner that had the stately Carlyle shaking his head in shame.

Half an hour later she was stalking down Curzon Street, a plump maid *and* a muscular footman trailing behind her. The last had been Carlyle's contribution, and as she was too in awe of him to refuse, she had said nothing. The lad, at least, kept his own counsel, which was more than could be said for Suzanne, who kept up a stream of chatter and criticism with every step.

"You ought not to be walking so fast, miss. You can not go in that shop, miss, it is too common. You mustn't lift your skirts so high when you cross the street, miss. I saw your petticoat that last time." And on and on, until Penelope was ready to shriek. Whatever dangers the streets of London posed to her person and her virtue, she did not think they could be any worse than listening to such lunatic ravings.

When they reached the bookshop, her temper was such that she dared not to speak except to order the loquacious maid to wait outside, in a manner that made anything other than obedience unthinkable. Satisfied at having finally silenced the wretched creature, she pushed open the door and hurried into the shop.

Inside she wasted little time in going to the section set aside for scientific literature. The book she had been hoping to find hadn't come in, but there was an excellent copy of Sir Humphry's lectures bound in gold-stamped leather. Only yesterday Daniel had expressed his admiration for the other man's brilliance, and on impulse she decided to buy it for him. She was approaching the clerk's desk when the door opened and Mr. Bellamy, accompanied by Miss Reynolds and an older woman, walked in.

"Good day to you, Miss Grantham," Mr. Bellamy said, offering her a courteous bow. "How are you this fine day?"

"Quite well, Mr. Bellamy, Miss Reynolds." She gave the younger lady an acknowledging smile. Miss Reynolds was wearing a cape of smoky-blue velvet with a matching bonnet perched on her blond curls, and she looked like a perfect, porcelain doll. That she noticed such a thing vexed Penelope, for it made her fear she was turning into the species of female who cared for nothing more than fashion. She had always scorned such females, and it was mortifying to think she had sunk so low as to join their ranks.

"I might have known we should find you here," Mr. Bellamy said, his manner as ebullient as Penelope remembered. "Chalmerstones is famous for their selection of scientific materials. Have you found anything interesting?"

Penelope showed them the book she'd selected. "It is for my brother," she said, smiling as she thought how pleased he would be. "He is a great admirer of Sir Humphry."

Miss Reynolds brightened at that. "Your brother?" she echoed, her gaze darting about the shop. "Is he here with you?"

"No, the book is meant as a surprise," Penelope replied politely, amused to note the other lady's infatuation with Daniel hadn't lessened. She couldn't wait until they were alone so that she could twig him about it.

They chatted for several minutes, and the conversation drifted to Miss Chartfield. Penelope mentioned she'd sent her a note asking permission to call, and Miss Reynolds exclaimed, "Oh, but you must call upon her this very afternoon, Miss Grantham! Thursday is her at-home day, and I know she would welcome a visit from you."

"Indeed?" Penelope asked hopefully.

Miss Reynolds have a vigorous nod, causing the silver plume adorning her bonnet to bob wildly. "She has her own scientific salon," she added, "and she was saying just this morning she thought you would make an excellent addition to our circle."

This information was balm to Penelope's soul, for this was precisely the sort of thing she had envisioned when she'd dreamed of coming to London. She was about to express her gratitude to Miss Reynolds when Mr. Bellamy gave a short bark of laughter.

"You'll note it was yourself who was invited to join this august group, and not your esteemed brother," he said with a mocking smile. "We lowly men are excluded from membership, as we are not considered sufficiently intelligent to join you ladies in your learned discussions."

"Just as well," the older woman, whom Miss Reynolds had introduced as Miss Jane Princeton, her companion, opined with a loud sniff. "You would only take the thing over and run it as you have everything else. This way the ladies will have some hope of expressing their opinions without interference."

"Yes, Marcus," Miss Reynolds's lips formed a pretty moue. "You gentlemen would hog the conversation all to yourselves, and we ladies would be reduced to discussing the weather. Is that not so, Miss Grantham?" She turned to Penelope for support.

"Or even more lowering still, we would be reduced to chatting about fashion," Penelope agreed, delighted by the misanthropic turn of the conversation. "And you mustn't be so hard on Miss Chartfield, sir. She is but paying the masculine world in the same coin with which you have always paid us.''

"What the deuce is that supposed to mean?" Mr. Bellamy
looked more than a little confused.

"Well," Penelope began, wondering how close she could
come to confessing all and still make her point. "Take the
way the scientific societies—even those which admit women
into membership—only permit men to apply for grants and
the like. Women are every bit as interested in scientific study
as men. Should we not be granted the same opportunity to
prove those theories? What of my own brother? If he were my
sister instead, would that make his work any less valid?"

"Of course not," Mr. Bellamy said, looking decidedly put
upon. "But that is a moot point. Ulysses is a man."

"But if he were not?" Penelope pressed. "Should he be
denied the monies for experimentation merely on account of
his gender?"

Mr. Bellamy opened his mouth as if to respond and then
closed it again, shaking his head with a wry chuckle. "I bow
to your debating skills, Miss Grantham," he said, inclining his
head to her. "Your superior logic has quite defeated me. What
a pity it is that ladies are also denied a voice in Parliament; I
daresay you would put all those dusty politicians to shame. Or
is it your contention that ladies should also be included in the
political process?" He sent her a challenging look.

"Considering that we are often the ones to pay the heaviest
price for the bills Parliament enacts, I would suppose that
would only be fair," Penelope retorted. She softened her
shocking remarks by adding, "But to be truthful, politics holds
little interest for me. Science is my true passion.

"May I ask why you seem so hipped by Miss Chartfield's
policy of allowing only ladies to join her circle?" she asked
after a moment, tilting her head to one side as she studied his
face. "Surely there is no dearth of similar societies for men?"

"Indeed there is not," he agreed with a laugh, "but unfortunately they are comprised mostly of dull old men. My cousin's circle, however, contains all of the prettiest, most witty
ladies, and I suppose I am annoyed at being denied the pleasure of flirting with all of you. It is too cruel by half."

Penelope was tempted to point out that ladies interested in

science would hardly be amenable to flirting, but she managed to control herself. She decided Mr. Bellamy's charm grew thin upon closer inspection, and concluded it was time to make a strategic retreat. Spying her maid and footman peering in the window at them, she gave them a small wave before turning to the others.

"I had best be on my way," she said, offering her apologies with a polite smile. "I promised mother I would only be gone a few minutes, and she worries when I am late."

"Will you and your brother be calling upon Lynette this afternoon?" Miss Reynolds asked, and then flushed a becoming shade of rose. "I thought I would ask so she would know whether or not to expect you," she added lamely.

Penelope arched an eyebrow, but held her tongue with what she considered commendable maturity. "I cannot answer for Ulysses, as I haven't spoken with him this morning," she informed the younger woman politely. "But my mother and I will make every effort to pay our respects. Is there any set time Miss Chartfield begins receiving callers?"

"She is at home any time after luncheon," Miss Princeton said, obviously to prevent her pretty charge from making an even bigger cake of herself. "She has already invited Georgina and me to stop by, so perhaps we shall see you there."

"And naturally I shall be there as well," Mr. Bellamy assured her with annoying joviality. "I wouldn't dream of missing one of my dear cousin's at-home days."

"I am sure you would not." Penelope's tone was falsely sweet. "I will look forward to seeing you there." She took her leave, wondering if even the pleasure of seeing Miss Chartfield would be worth the price of her encroaching cousin's company.

" 'Tis about time you were getting here. I was beginning to think my message to you had gone astray," Polson said, his blue eyes filled with reproach as he watched Daniel sliding into the booth opposite him.

"We were out late last night, and my valet didn't think to give me your note until this morning," Daniel replied coolly, his wary gaze sweeping the taproom's smoky interior before he settled against the back of the wooden booth. "Now, what news have you of Lord Haworth? Your note said it was important."

"Aye, that it is," Polson agreed, lowering his gaze to the pewter mug of ale cradled in his beefy hands. He moved the mug from one hand to the other before speaking.

"I went up to York as you asked, and did a bit of poking about. I found a stablehand, name of Phillips; he is willing to swear, under oath, that he saw the marquess and your brother fighting on the day before he was killed."

Daniel felt as if he had just taken a blow to the head. "What?" he asked in disbelief.

Polson repeated his story, adding the further information that it had taken this Phillips and two other servants to pull the two men apart. When he finished speaking, it was all Daniel could do to keep his voice low.

"Did this Phillips inform the authorities of what happened?" he asked, a cold knot of fury forming in his stomach.

"And run afoul of his master?" Polson raised a gray eyebrow mockingly. "And in any case, he saw no reason to say anything at the time. Like everyone else, he thought Richard's death naught but an accident. It was only later, after he heard of James's death, that he began to wonder."

The knot in Daniel's belly grew tighter. "Why did he tell you?" he asked, feeling a deadly calm stealing over him. "Did you offer him money?"

"I paid him for the information, to be sure," Polson admitted with an expansive shrug, "but only after he offered it of his own free will. He's left the marquess's employ, and is hoping to make his way out of the country."

Daniel's brows met in a frown. "Why should he want to do that? Is he afraid of Haworth?"

"Remember I told you it took two other men to break up the fight between his lordship and Richard?" Polson asked. At Daniel's nod he said, "Well, it seems one of the other men drowned in an unfortunate accident not three months past, and now t'other one is nowhere to be found. Phillips mightn't be the brightest lad you'd ever hope to be speaking with, but he's no half-wit, either. He's that scared, I can tell you."

A pert serving girl appeared with a mug for Daniel, and he welcomed the distraction she provided. It gave him time to organize his thoughts and master the killing rage that had settled deep in his soul. The moment they were alone again, he pushed his ale aside without tasting it.

"Do you know where Phillips is now?" he asked, leaning his elbows on the table's scarred surface and meeting Polson's eyes.

"I thought you might be wishing a word with him, so I left him at the estate with one of your old retainers."

Daniel considered that for a moment, and then dug into his pocket for a handful of bank notes. "I want him brought to London—discreetly, mind," he added, handing Polson the money. "If Haworth suspects we are on to him and starts searching this Phillips out, it is logical to assume our property will be the first place he will look."

Polson pocketed the money with a nod. "I hadn't thought of that, but I daresay you are right. He's a devilishly clever cove, from what I've been hearing."

"I know," Daniel said grimly, thinking of the information he had already uncovered. He hadn't yet had the dubious pleasure of making the marquess's acquaintance, but from what he had learned, his lordship's reputation was not all that it should be. He was considered to be a rake and a rattle by a society which usually doted on such vices, and it was whispered some of the sterner mamas had already scratched his name from their lists of eligible suitors. It wasn't the scandal he'd hoped to uncover, but at least it gave him some measure of the man he was investigating.

"Does Phillips know what the fight was about?" he asked, picking up his mug and taking a thoughtful sip.

"He said he caught but a few words, but it was his impression the quarrel was over money. He said Richard even mentioned an amount: ten thousand pounds."

Daniel choked on his ale. "Ten thousand!" he gasped, setting his tankard down with a thump. "Is he certain?"

"Fair certain," Polson said. "And it was his impression that it was the marquess as owed the money to Richard."

Daniel thrust his hand through his hair, trying to think.

When he'd set out to learn the truth of his brothers' deaths, the last thing he'd expected was that he would develop proof of possible murder so quickly. Now that he'd done so, he hadn't a clue what his next move should be.

"What of James?" he asked at last, pushing his tangle of emotions to one side. "Was he aware of the debt Haworth owed?"

"If he did, he never mentioned the matter to me," Polson replied. Then he frowned. "Although now that you talk of it, I don't think he did know. Jarvidge, he was your brother's solicitor, he showed me a list of the debts and assets Richard left behind when he died, and nowhere did I see such an amount set down. I'd remember it if I had."

Daniel thought of his brother's mania for order, and his frown deepened. "What of Richard's personal papers? Was there anything there?" he asked, refusing to believe Richard would have allowed such an asset to go unrecorded.

"Jarvidge went over everything with Master James and Andrew following Richard's death," Polson answered, shaking his head. "There was nothing."

Daniel remained silent for several more moments and then shook his head. "Damn, but this is deep," he muttered in frustration. "If Haworth did owe Richard ten thousand pounds why is there no record of it? And if he didn't owe him the money, why the devil would he want to kill him? And what of James? What possible reason would the marquess have for harming him?"

"I don't know, Mr. Warfield . . . Mr. Grantham," Polson corrected, his expression bleak. "None of it makes the slightest bit of sense, to be sure, and yet . . ."

"Yet?" Daniel pressed when Polson did not continue.

"And yet when you think on it, it makes more sense than believing the whole of everything is mere happenstance," the other man concluded, his mouth set in a grim line. "Let us assume Haworth did kill Richard in a moment of panic, thinking that would erase the debt. It wouldn't take him long to realize the debt would just pass to James, and that would mean he'd have no choice but to take care of him as well. Now he is making friends with young Andrew, and—"

A thrill of fear shot through Daniel. "What are you talking about?" he demanded harshly. "I haven't heard anything to indicate Andrew and Haworth are anything beyond acquaintances!"

"That is so, but according to his secretary, Mr. Stephens, the marquess has been burying the lad in invitations these past weeks. Until now his lordship has always sent his regrets, but last night he accompanied Haworth to his club for a night of drinking and gaming. Today it's Tattersall's they're off to, as if the viscount would know one end of a horse from the other," Polson added, shaking his head with an indulgent chuckle. "Meaning no disrespect to your brother, sir."

Daniel said nothing. Once he would have accepted Polson's estimation of his brother without comment, but having seen Andrew after so many years, he wasn't so certain. Despite his youthful appearance, there was a hardness and cool intelligence about him that made Daniel think there was more to him than Polson realized.

"What of the other task I set for you?" he asked, deciding he would puzzle the matter out later when he was alone. "Were you able to do as I asked?"

"Aye, that I was." Polson gave another chuckle, reaching into his great coat for a letter which he handed to Daniel. "And might I say, sir, 'twas no easy thing for an Irishman like myself to go hat in hand to the king's own minister on your behalf and beg an audience with the Regent."

Daniel flicked open the thick document, his eyes glimmering in satisfaction as he read the formally worded invitation to attend his royal highness at Carlton House. "Polson, you are a pearl beyond price," he said, raising his gaze long enough to send the steward a smile. "I thank you for your heroic efforts."

"Happy to have been of service." Polson inclined his head with a cheeky grin. "If you don't mind my asking, why should you be wishing to see that great overfed babe? 'Tis not as if he commands any real power in the government."

"No," Daniel agreed, tucking the letter in his pocket. "But he does command something of immense value to me."

"And what might that be?" Polson seemed genuinely puzzled.

"That is something I prefer keeping to myself—for the moment, at least, " Daniel said, reaching for his ale. "Tell me of Burlington Manor. Is everything all right?"

Polson spent the next half hour filling Daniel in on all that had transpired during his long absence. He was relieved to hear the estate was still prospering, although that relief was tempered by the knowledge no improvements had been made since prior to his father's death. He pressed Polson for more information, and the other man gave a dispirited sigh.

"Right you are to ask," he said, folding his arms across his chest and looking grim. "I've mentioned the matter to his lordship any number of times, but he'll hear naught of it. 'The sheep and oats are your province, Polson,' he'll tell me, and then dash out to spend a hundred pounds on a hunter. Ah, well." His shoulders moved in a philosophical shrug. "The lad's young yet; he'll learn."

Daniel kept his silence with an effort. At Andrew's age he'd been on his own in a foreign land, earning his living through the sweat of his brow. There had been no fine title, no family fortune to soften his way; and he realized now that had been the making of him. Perhaps all Andrew required was a chance to prove himself, Daniel brooded.

He started as he realized Polson was addressing him. "My apologies, Polson, I fear I was not attending. What was it you said?"

The steward regarded him a long moment before responding. "I was asking, sir, if you've given any thought to claiming the title? Whatever your quarrel with your father, you *are* Viscount Burlington. You've a responsibility to the estate, and to the people living there. They depend upon you for their livelihood, and leaving a half-green boy in charge is not fair to them. It's not fair, my lord."

The reference to his station was a deliberate challenge; a challenge Daniel accepted in stoic silence. He had already given the matter a great deal of thought, and his answer was the same as it had been that day in the cemetery.

"Daniel Warfield had an obligation to the title," he said,

his voice even as he met Polson's gaze. "But to all intents and purposes, Daniel Warfield is dead. The title is Andrew's, and I will not take it from him."

"But sir—"

"No," Daniel interrupted, his voice low and intense as he leaned over the table. "Listen to me, Polson. I am an American now. I have another life, and once my business is England is completed I am returning home. I am resolved on this, and I will not be swayed by your talk of loyalty and responsibility. My father had a responsibility to me as well, and he turned his back on that responsibility without so much as batting an eye."

Polson looked taken aback, but then said, "What of your brothers? Do you owe them nothing as well?"

The quiet words were like the lash of a whip across Daniel's soul. "I owe them a great deal," he said, forcing the words past his clenched teeth, "and I mean to repay that debt by avenging their deaths. But that is the extent of what I owe. Once that has been done I shall be leaving, and nothing you do or say shall convince me otherwise."

Polson regarded him silently. "You sound fair set on this," he said at last.

"I am," Daniel assured him grimly.

"Then I shall say no more of it," Polson said, his lips lifting in a wry smile. "I'm Irish, and who better than we know a lost cause when we see it? But"—he met Daniel's gaze— "when all of this is over, I want you to speak with Andrew. Beneath his youthful ways he's a good man, I'm sure of it, and it's only a bit of direction he is wanting. Give him the guidance young Robert tried giving you, and if need be, give him a quick kick to his backside as well. Think about it, Daniel, that is all I am asking."

8

By the following Wednesday Penelope was so vexed she was ready to shriek. To her annoyance she, or rather, *Ulysses*, had become Society's Darling, and every day's post brought a fresh avalanche of invitations. Her mama was in high alt, enjoying their new-found popularity with childlike abandon, and Penelope's vociferous complaints fell on increasingly deaf ears. Wail or threaten how she might, each night found her at some ball or soiree, watching in disgust as titled ladies and their nubile daughters collected around Daniel as if he were a pasha and they his willing harem.

And the men were every bit as bad, she brooded, glowering down at the flames dancing in the hearth. One would think Daniel was the Oracle at Delphi the way they clung to his every word, muttering "How true!" and "I have always thought as much" every time the treacherous beast shared one of *her* theories.

Even the controversy involving Dr. Baker's allegations that his friend, Mr. Collister, was claiming Ulysses's work as his own, did not dim the enthusiasm with which Daniel was received. If anything, it only added to it, as everyone in London seemed eager to align themselves with "the brilliant young scientist so wrongly slandered," as one of the morning journals put it.

Telling herself none of this was Daniel's fault, and that in truth he was doing her a great service, no longer had any discernible effect upon Penelope's temper. Enough was enough, and the moment Daniel returned from his mysterious errand she meant to make it plain that, whatever agreement they might have had in the past, it was she who would be in charge from now on.

That was another thing, she thought, picking up the poker and giving the fire a vicious jab. Daniel had taken to disappearing for hours at a time without so much as a by-your-leave to explain where he had gone, and her maid had let slip he was constantly receiving mysterious *billet-doux*. Something was clearly afoot, she decided sourly, and whatever that something was, she was determined to put an end to it.

She was just about to ring for Carlyle to demand further intelligence on her ersatz brother's whereabouts when the door opened and Daniel walked in, his face set in the cold, distant lines Penelope was coming to loath.

"Carlyle informed me you wished to speak with me," he said, studying her down the length of his nose. "What is it?"

Penelope glared at him for several seconds before saying, "Are you aware, sir, that it is an established fact of physics, that when a man's sense of self-importance grows larger than his intellect, the sheer weight of said self-importance will simply topple him over?"

His green eyes narrowed. "What?"

"Oh yes," she gave a vigorous nod. "I believe it has to do with the principles of stress, although architecture has never been my strong suit. I read a treatise by Michelangelo and he—"

"What the devil are you prattling on about?" Daniel interrupted, his expression thunderous as he advanced upon her.

Penelope stood her ground. "I was but making a scientific observation."

He stopped a few inches from her, and it was obvious from the set of his jaw that he was making a heroic effort to hold his temper in check. "What is it you wished to discuss?" he asked, his voice low and controlled.

His question set Penelope's teeth even further on edge, and for a moment she toyed with the notion of letting her own temper slip the reins. She was spoiling for a brangle, and she found the admission most humiliating. She prided herself on her cool intellect, and yet with Daniel she was at the mercy of a dozen conflicting emotions.

"Penelope? I am waiting."

The clipped reminder punctured her desire for control and she brought her chin up in defiant pride. "I am very hipped with you," she announced, folding her arms across her chest and fixing him with a stern look.

His lips curved in response. "I could tell," he replied in the mocking drawl she found so attractive. "What heinous crime have I committed this time?"

She knew he was attempting to placate her, but she refused to be charmed. "I haven't time to list your shortcomings," she said, lowering her arms with a regal sniff. "I merely wished to inform you I won't be attending the Fitzroys' ball this evening."

The indulgent laughter faded from his eyes. "May I ask why?"

"Because I don't wish to," she said, ignoring the cold flatness in his voice. "I told you when we first started that I cared little for society, and I meant what I said. You were good enough to help me and I have done my best to oblige you, but I have decided I have had enough. From now on I wish to devote myself to more intellectual pursuits."

"I see," he said, his expression giving no indication as to his thoughts. "Have you a reason for this decision, or are you merely being obstinate?"

Penelope was momentarily taken aback by the naked challenge in his words. In the past Daniel had often been vexing and top-lofty, but this was the first time he'd been so deliberately provocative. It was almost as if he wanted to cause a quarrel between them, and even though she'd been aching for just such a fight only moments before, she realized such a confrontation would accomplish nothing. If she hoped to convince him of her sincerity, she couldn't let her temper get the best of her.

"It is rather difficult to explain," she began, walking over to the fireplace where a collection of painted porcelain figurines were arranged on the mantelpiece. She picked up her favorite piece, a shepherdess, and ran her finger over the girl's smiling features, struggling to put into words feelings that were as nebulous as river mist.

"I am a scientist," she said. "And I know more about elements and properties than I do the correct way to hold a cup of tea, or the proper way to address a bishop."

"I haven't seen you make a mistake," Daniel replied, his voice guarded. "In fact, I find your manners quite delightful."

His lack of understanding filled her with frustration. "That is precisely my point!" she cried, replacing the shepherdess with a thump and whirling around to confront him. "They're not *my* manners! They are the dictates placed upon me by society, and I abhor them!

"Don't you see?" she added, desperate to make him understand. "I don't belong here! I hate all this folderol: the concern with one's position, the endless discussion of fashion. Yesterday I actually had a conversation about ribbons, and I enjoyed it!" To her shame her eyes filled with tears. "I am losing myself, Daniel. I am becoming the sort of woman I swore I would never be."

There was a tense silence, then Daniel moved forward to take her gently in his arms. She buried her face against his chest, clinging to him for refuge from the emotional storm waging inside her.

"Shhh." His hand moved soothingly over her hair as he held her. "It's all right, Penelope; do not cry."

"I'm not crying," she denied with a sniff, unconsciously pressing closer to his comforting warmth. "It's just you don't know what it is like to be forced into a mold you despise. To have everyone around you determined to make you into that which you do not wish to be."

His hand stilled in her hair, and she felt him stiffen as if in pain. Fearing she'd embarrassed him with her tears, she lifted her head from his shoulder and took a hasty step back.

"What a simpleton you must think me," she said, brushing a hand over her cheek. "You must know I'm usually not so missish."

His expression was so hard it might have been carved from

stone. "I know," he said, his voice oddly strained.

"I daresay it is naught but a case of nerves," she babbled on, hiding her chagrin behind a shaky laugh. "Our presentation is in a little over a fortnight, and I am beginning to fear we shall never be ready in time."

Daniel hesitated a moment before replying. "I have been meaning to discuss that with you," he said, his eyes not quite meeting hers. "I have had a note from Mr. Whitley of the Royal Society, and he has arranged for one of their laboratories to be placed at my disposal. If you wish, we could go there tomorrow afternoon and work on the experiment. Unless you have other plans?" he added, sending her a questioning look.

As it happened she'd made arrangements with Miss Chartfield to visit the other lady's modiste, but she didn't think that signified. Mere velvets and lace could in no way compare to the lure of the finest laboratories in the country.

"None at all," she assured him, composing a note of apology in her mind. "What time do you wish to leave? After breakfast?"

Again there was a slight hesitation before Daniel spoke. "Not so early as that. I have . . . other obligations in the morning I must honor. But I should be home in time for a quick bite of nuncheon. Shall we say two o'clock?"

Two o'clock sounded like forever to Penelope, but she supposed she could wait if she must. She also wondered what other obligations would take up Daniel's entire morning, but she was too excited to pursue the matter. "Two o'clock will be fine," she assured him. "I'll go over my notes tonight and draw up a list of experiments for us to perform. I read an interesting article on the use of mercury as a conducting agent and—"

"Penelope," Daniel interrupted, his tone surprisingly solemn, "I am afraid I must insist you attend the Fitzroys' ball tonight. You must know this isn't something I ask lightly," he added before she could protest. "I promise in future I shall do what I can to accommodate your wishes, but tonight I need you there."

Penelope gazed up at him in bewilderment. "But why?"

she demanded, genuinely puzzled. "Why should it matter one way or another if I am there?"

Daniel remained silent, as if searching for the proper words to explain. "Do you recall my mentioning a Lord Haworth?"

"Who?" Her brows knit as she struggled to recall the name.

"George Henry Alistair, the Marquess of Haworth. I believe I mentioned him as a possible patron."

"Oh," Penelope said, vaguely remembering the conversation. "Yes, I suppose I recall your making mention of him, but I still do not see what that has to do with me. You are the one who must need court his favor."

"Perhaps," he agreed, "but as I am doing it for you, the least you can do is to be there to flutter your lashes at him."

Penelope took instant exception to this. "I do not flutter my lashes at any man!"

"Then talk his leg off about copper's properties as a magnetic coil," Daniel said, showing that if nothing else, he had been reading the materials she had given him. "It isn't necessary that he fall in love with you, Penelope; it is only necessary that you be there. Please," he added, sounding so desperate that she capitulated with a disgruntled sigh.

"Oh, very well. But I expect some consideration in return. I meant what I said about not wishing to participate in society any more than necessary, and if I attend the Fitzroys' tiresome ball, I insist I be allowed out of whatever function I choose for the rest of the week. Agreed?"

He looked as if he would argue the point, but then shrugged. "Agreed," he said, capturing her hand and giving it a firm shake. "Thank you, ma'am; I am in your debt."

The feel of his hand clasping hers made Penelope's pulse race, and she freed her hand as quickly as she could. "I should say you are," she said, striving for calm and praying he hadn't guessed his touch had discomfited her. "And you may make sure I intend holding you to that debt."

A rare glint of laughter shone in Daniel's eyes. "I am sure you shall," he drawled, his lips curving in a smile. "You drive as hard a bargain as any Yankee trader, and I am grateful not to find myself rolled up horse, gun, and blanket. Goodbye, Penelope; I look forward to seeing you this evening."

* * *

"Will there be anything else, Mr. Grantham?" Daniel's valet queried, his manner solicitous as he studied his handiwork with a critical eye. "If you do not care for your cravat, I should be happy to tie another in a different style."

It took a moment for the question to penetrate the black fog filling Daniel's mind. He emerged long enough to give his reflection a cursory examination, then shook his head. "Everything is fine, Frederick," he said, dismissing the valet with a shrug. "You may go now."

"Are you certain?" The valet stood on tiptoe to brush a fleck of dust from the shoulders of Daniel's evening coat. "You mentioned earlier you most particularly wished to look your best this evening, and I would not like to think you are in any way dissatisfied with my performance."

Daniel heard the genuine concern in the man's voice, and turned once more to survey himself in the cheval glass. He'd been in London long enough to realize his black velvet jacket and tight-fitting satin breeches were in the first stare of fashion, and he doubted even the Beau himself could find fault in his elegantly arranged cravat. He looked the very tulip, he thought cynically, and the admission was enough to make him scowl.

You don't know what it is like to be forced into a mold you despise. To have everyone around you determined to make you into that which you do not wish to be.

Penelope's anguished words echoed in his mind, and he remembered the battles he and his father had often waged over his wardrobe. His father had insisted he dress in the same somber manner as he and Robert favored, which only made him that much more resolved to dress as outlandishly as possible. He hadn't been a macaroni . . . precisely, but there were a few waistcoats and jackets he now winced to recall. Had he really worn a brocade waistcoat with gold and purple roses embroidered on it? he wondered, mentally shaking his head at such youthful folly.

"Sir?" Frederick was fluttering nervously at his side. "Is there anything further you require?"

The valet's anxious voice recalled Daniel to the present, and he scraped up a quick smile. "No, all is perfection, I promise you," he said reassuringly. "If I appear distracted, it is because I have other concerns on my mind at the moment. I did not mean to imply you had done less than your usual sterling job. You are a wonder, Frederick; I should be lost without you."

Frederick's chest puffed out at Daniel's effusive praise. "I am delighted to know my poor efforts have found favor with you, Mr. Grantham," he said, sketching a courtly bow. "And if I may say, it is a pleasure serving you. 'Tis plain you are a true gentleman; unlike some of my former patrons," he added, his peaked nose wrinkling in a delicate grimace.

Some of Daniel's pleasure faded at the remark. "Thank you, Frederick," he said, wondering how much a gentleman the other man would think him if he knew of the charade he was enacting. "It is kind of you to say so."

"Not at all, sir," the valet assured him earnestly. "And upon that note, there is something I have been wishing to discuss with you. I am sure it is nothing, but I should feel remiss in my duties were I not to bring the matter to your attention."

The hair on the back of Daniel's neck prickled at the distress in Frederick's voice. "What is it?"

"I would not wish you to think I am in the habit of imbibing in my off-duty hours," the valet began anxiously, eager, it seemed, to make a clean breast of things. "Nor would I want you believing I am the sort to frequent taverns and the like, but—"

"Cut line, Frederick," Daniel interrupted, his patience thinning. "I don't give a tinker's damn what you do on your own time; just get on with whatever you are trying to tell me."

"As you wish, sir," Frederick bobbed his head. "I was at an inn . . . a most respectable establishment, frequented by those in service to the great houses, when I chanced to meet an old friend—Thomas Gilforth. We served in the same household when we were lads, and I heard he'd gone on to join Viscount Burlington's household as underbutler."

The mention of his brother's name made Daniel stiffen. "Go on," he said cautiously.

"Naturally, as it had been some years since last we spoke,

we fell to discussing our current positions,'' Frederick continued in his verbose manner. "He seemed to feel it necessary to touch rather repeatedly on the fact that his master was a member of the *ton* and a noted whipster in the bargain, and I responded by telling him of the many honors accorded you because of your scientific experiments. Tom feigned disinterest at first, so I felt compelled to convince him you were in every way equal, if not superior, to his employer. It was only upon reflection that I realized how much I had let slip with my foolish bragging.''

The coil of tension tightened in Daniel's stomach. "What sort of things?'' he asked, steeling himself for the answer.

"Nothing as to bring shame upon you, sir,'' Frederick assured him earnestly. "I am a gentleman's gentleman, after all, and I am sure I know better than to spread false tales about my employer. I merely told him what a fine gentleman you are, and how you had won *entree* to the highest level of society. I also made mention of your association with several scientific organizations, and the fact you would be performing an experiment in front of the Royal Society itself. That did seem to knock him back apace,'' he added, looking smug.

None of what Frederick had let slip so far sounded that awful to Daniel, yet the very fact Andrew was apparently checking on him could not be discounted. "Did this Thomas ask any particular sort of questions about me?'' he asked, wondering if there was time to send Polson a hasty message.

To his alarm a delicate flush stole across Frederick's cheeks. "That is the odd part, Mr. Grantham. He seemed most particularly interested in learning if there was any servant gossip about your . . . your birth.''

"My birth?''

"Yes.'' Frederick's flush grew even more pronounced. "He kept asking if I had ever heard any whisper that . . . well, to be blunt, sir, that you are not your father's son.''

The blood drained from Daniel's face. "What?'' he exclaimed incredulously.

Frederick gave a mute nod. "My very reaction, sir. I assured the forward fellow that your mother was the embodiment of all that was proper, but he kept pressing the matter. He wanted to know how old you were, the place of your birth, where you were raised; that sort of thing. He even asked if I had access to such information, and that was when I decided to take my leave of him. I—I trust you are not angry with me?'' he said, sending Daniel a timid look.

Daniel shook his head. ''Not at all,'' he said, forcing himself to sound indifferent. ''I am glad you brought the matter to my notice. When did this happen?''

''Friday last,'' Frederick said, bundling up his brushes and combs in preparation for his departure. ''I debated whether or not I should tell you, and had we not spoken, I was going to go to Mr. Carlyle and seek his counsel.''

The last thing Daniel wanted was the chance any of this might get back to Penelope. She was already far too curious about his past as it was, and he dared not risk that Andrew's questions would spark more of her own. ''I am glad you did not,'' he said, giving his valet a stern look. ''In fact, you are not to discuss this with any other member of this household, is that understood? I don't want word of this man's insinuations getting back to my mother,'' he added at the valet's look of affront. ''She would be mortified were she to hear of it.''

''You may be quite sure I shan't discuss anything with the lower orders,'' he assured Daniel earnestly. ''I should never dream of doing such a thing.''

''I am sure you would not,'' Daniel said, reaching an abrupt decision. ''But in the meanwhile, I want you to keep your ears open to the other servants' tattle. If you discover any of them have been similarly questioned, you are to notify me at once.''

''Of course, sir,'' Frederick promised, looking properly shocked. ''Do you think there is any such possibility?''

''I do not know,'' Daniel admitted grimly. ''But I intend finding out.''

To Daniel's relief Penelope appeared downstairs at the appointed hour, looking fetching in a new gown of purple and gold striped satin. Her dark blond hair was covered by a dashing aigrette, fashioned with two white plumes fastened to the front with a glittering array of rhinestones. He gave her a warm smile as he settled her matching silk shawl about her shoulders.

"At the risk of incurring your wrath, ma'am, may I say how lovely you look tonight? That is a stunning ensemble."

As expected, his compliment made her wrinkle her pert nose in disgust. "I look like a hopeful chit making her bows to a highly eligible duke," she grumbled, although her hazel eyes were sparkling. "I am glad I am so sadly aged, otherwise I should have to wear those insipid whites and pastels Mama assures me are the rage amongst the debs. A fine cake I should look then."

"Who says you are sadly aged?" he asked, feigning anger as she pulled on her evening gloves. "Give me his name and I shall call him to accounts at once."

"Dolt." Despite her sharp words her cheeks were flushed with pleasure. "As if any man should say such a thing."

"Ah, then it was a lady who dared disparage you," he said, enjoying their nonsensical chatter. It made a pleasant counterpoint for his dark thoughts. "No doubt she is jealous of your success with the beaus, and means to slander your good name. Who is she? I shall make sure to cut her quite dead should we meet; that should teach her to wag her spiteful tongue."

Penelope looked startled for a moment and then tossed back her head and laughed. She was still chuckling when Mrs. Grantham joined them. "You wouldn't believe what a coxcomb this wretch has become," she said, shooting Daniel a teasing glance as they climbed into the waiting carriage. "He believes withholding his attentions is enough to cast any female into the sulks."

"Oh, I can think of a chit or two who could be counted upon to shed a few bitter tears," Mrs. Grantham remarked, regarding them both with maternal pride. "Ulysses is quite popular amongst the ladies, and you are not without your admirers, you know."

"Pooh, clever schoolboys and brooding poets, the lot of them," Penelope sniffed, dismissing her suitors with a pretty shrug. "I find them excessively boring."

"You would," Daniel said, although he made a mental note to pay closer mind to Penelope's swains. He'd been so lost in his own affairs of late that he had failed to pay any attention the men fluttering about her. Clearly he would have to do a better job in future, he decided, assuring himself it was no less than any loving brother would do for a younger sister.

The Fitzroys' house was on Cleveland Row, and as their carriage struggled through traffic, Daniel and Mrs. Grantham discussed the guests who would be present that evening.

"Of course," Mrs. Grantham opined, fanning herself languidly, "not all the guests are what I would call good *ton.* For some reason I can not fathom, Sally has seen fit to invite that awful Haworth to make up our numbers, and he is such a loose screw I shouldn't be in the least surprised to hear several families with marriageable daughters will cry off. The world knows him for an unprincipled fortune hunter. Ah, well, perhaps she only did so to insure Lord Burlington would attend. The two have been quite close of late."

"Haworth?" The satin of Penelope's gown rustled as she sat forward. "The Marquess of Haworth, do you mean?"

"Of course," her mother said, bending a suspicious frown on Penelope. "Never say you know his lordship?"

Daniel felt Penelope's startled gaze resting on his face. "Not I," she admitted, "but Daniel—"

"I believe I mentioned the name to Penelope in passing," Daniel interrupted swiftly, hoping to forestall Penelope from saying anything further. "But at the time I did not know he had such a blackened reputation."

"Oh, it is more than black," Mrs. Grantham said, obviously delighted to pass on such titillating gossip. "He is said to be deep in Dun territory, and looking to repair his fortunes by fair means or foul."

"So are half the men one meets at Almack's," Penelope said, clearly bored with the conversation. "Why should his lordship be regarded any differently? Did he kill someone?" And she laughed at her own witticism.

Daniel held his breath, waiting for Mrs. Grantham to reply. "Well, there are *stories*," she allowed, her fan stilling. "There was an unpleasant bit of business surrounding a . . . er . . . a female engaged in a certain occupation, who is said to have disappeared after having a row with his lordship. And then there was the mystery surrounding the death of the previous

Lord Burlington while he was visiting Haworth's estate in Yorkshire. Nothing was ever proven, but there was no end to the rumors.''

Daniel could not have been more stunned had the older woman hit him over the head with her reticule. "What rumors?" he asked at last, forcing himself to lean back against the squabs and cross his feet. "I have heard nothing.''

"Because you do not sit on the dowager's bench," Mrs. Grantham said, sounding pleased. "The ladies there make it their business to keep their ears to the ground, and there is no morsel of gossip so small as to escape their notice.''

"But what is being said?" Daniel had to bite his lip to keep from shouting the question.

"Merely that it is odd a noted rider like Burlington should die in a riding accident," Mrs. Grantham answered, fanning herself once more. "And then not a year later, James, the fifth Viscount Burlington, died of a fever while Haworth was visiting the estate. You remember that Penelope, don't you?''

"Vaguely," Penelope admitted. "I remember Ulysses became convinced it was the plague, and made cook burn some foul-smelling herbs to keep the disease at bay.''

"Penelope!" Mrs. Grantham reproved her daughter with a gasp.

"Well, he did." As usual, Penelope sounded unrepentant. "But I do not understand. If there is any speculation at all Haworth had anything to do with the two brothers' deaths, then why ever should the present viscount have anything to do with him? I should think he would want to keep as far from him as possible. Or better still, that he would want to put a bullet through him.''

"Such inclinations, Penelope, are unbecoming in a Christian woman," Mrs. Grantham informed her sternly. "And this is not France, you know, where a man's head may be lopped off at the merest whisper of wrongdoing. As to the young viscount taking up with the marquess, I am sure he must have his reasons.''

Daniel remained silent through an act of sheer will. In a few short minutes he'd learned more than he had in a week of painstaking digging, but he was afraid to probe any further. The marquess and Andrew were supposed to be strangers to him, and he feared if he pressed too hard, Penelope would be certain to ask why. Her mind was every bit as sharp as her tongue, and he was not about to provide her with a reason to turn that incisive mind in his direction.

He settled quietly in his corner of the coach, contributing only enough to the conversation to keep the ladies from becoming suspicious. But even as he was commenting on the chances of the regent honoring the gathering with an appearance, he was deciding what he would do with what he had just learned.

It was probably just as well he did, for the first person to accost him upon his arrival was Andrew. Nor was he alone. Standing beside him, a superior smirk pinned to his lips, was none other than the notorious marquess of Haworth.

9

"Ah, Mr. Grantham, how nice to see you." Andrew's voice was cool as his light green gaze skimmed over Daniel's face. "I did say we would meet again, did I not?"

"So you did, my lord," Daniel replied, masking his emotions as he bowed his head. He turned and fixed the black-haired man standing beside Andrew with a pointed stare. "Sir, I do not believe I have had the pleasure?" he said, the bile rising in his throat as he realized he could be very well be staring into the face of his brothers' killer.

"My lord, allow me to make you known to Mr. Ulysses Grantham, a neighbor of mine from Bibury. Mr. Grantham, I should like to present you to his lordship, the marquess of Haworth," Andrew said, performing the introductions with languid grace. "And Haworth, these lovely ladies standing beside Mr. Grantham are his mother, Mrs. Grantham, and his sister, Miss Prudence, is it not?" He gave Penelope a charming smile which she returned, albeit slowly.

"Actually I am called Penelope," she said, curtseying as she offered first Andrew and then Haworth her hand. "But Prudence is my second name, my lord, so you are not far off the mark."

"You must forgive Andrew, Miss Grantham," Haworth drawled, his dark gaze resting on Penelope's face. "He was doubtlessly so taken by your charms his poor mind was quite rattled. I trust you shall forgive him, ma'am?''

Daniel saw Penelope's teeth fasten to her bottom lip before she replied. "I shall certainly try, sir," she said, lowering her lashes demurely.

Obviously pleased with her response, Haworth next turned his attention to Penelope's mother. "Mrs. Grantham, may I say what an honor it is to meet a needlewoman of your accomplishments?" he asked, taking her hand and bowing deeply. "I saw the stunning tapestry hanging in the grand hallway at Burlington, and was told you had been instrumental in its repair. Is that so?"

Mrs. Grantham blinked in surprise. "Why, yes, so it is," she said, her plump cheeks flushing with pleasure. "Tapestries are something of a hobby of mine, and I was more than happy to help when his lordship first approached me about it."

"Indeed?" The marquess appeared genuinely interested. "Then talent is something which clearly must run in your family. I had occasion to read your son's last article, and I must say I am surprised to find him so young. One would think a man of such genius would have a few gray hairs in his beard, what? Although after having met you, I now wonder that he should be so old. You are entirely too young to be the mother of so accomplished a gentleman.

"And Mr. Grantham, I must tell you that I am quite looking forward to your demonstration at the Royal Society." Daniel was the next recipient of Haworth's oily charm. "I would not worry about those tiresome claims being made by that Collister fellow. He is doubtlessly an ill-bred ruffian who is but jealous of the attention you have gained."

"Your lordship honors me," Daniel murmured, puzzled by Haworth's performance. So far he had behaved with surprising gentility for the black-hearted rake he was reputed to be, and he could not decide what to make of him.

"No, no, it is you who honor us, sir," Haworth assured him heartily. "I was telling Burlington here only yesterday that it is past time we began paying closer mind to the scientists among us. A few years ago gaslight was naught but a fanciful aspiration, and now it lights our way home. Who knows what other miracles await us, eh?"

They might have stood there exchanging pleasantries indefinitely, but for the press of people queuing up behind them. The sheer size of the crowd forced them out of the entryway and up the grand staircase, where they were greeted by their host and hostess, and in the confusion they lost sight of Andrew and the marquess. Daniel wasn't worried, as he'd already accomplished his primary goal of meeting Haworth. Now he could proceed at his own pace and plan what his next move should be.

"Ugh, I must say I am glad to have lost the marquess," Penelope remarked, glancing about the ballroom. "Had he dumped any more butter on us, I daresay we should have drowned."

Daniel shot her a startled look, both amused and relieved by her tart observation. He was beginning to doubt his own responses to Haworth, and it eased his mind to know she shared his opinion of the marquess.

"Penelope, that was most unkind of you!" Mrs. Grantham said reprovingly, slapping Penelope's arm with her fan. "I thought his lordship was most attentive."

Daniel and Penelope exchanged stunned looks at the abrupt *volte-face*. "Mama! What are you saying?" Penelope was the first to recover from the shock. "Not fifteen minutes ago, you were warning me against him in no uncertain terms!"

"I am sure I did not!" Mrs. Grantham denied, going quite red in the face.

"You told us he was beyond the pale, and that there were rumors he was all but a murderer," Daniel reminded her, horrified to think his temporary parent could be so easily gulled.

Mrs. Grantham fixed him with a quelling look. "Rumors, dear boy, not facts; I do believe I was quite clear on that point," she said severely. "And in any case, I can see the stories are exaggerated. No man who is interested in tapestries could possibly be involved in anything so base as murder."

"Well, he was much too fawning for my liking." Penelope's sniff did much to relieve Daniel's mind. "I hope he keeps his distance, although I am sure I need not worry. If he is on the catch for a fortune as you say, Mama, it is doubtful he will waste his time on a penniless nobody like me."

The arrival of Miss Chartfield and a pink-faced captain in the uniform of the Scots Grays prevented Mrs. Grantham from taking up the cudgels any further in Haworth's defense. Once the captain had been properly introduced as one of Miss Chartfield's numerous cousins, Mrs. Grantham excused herself, leaving the two couples to their own devices. The captain's face grew even pinker as he asked Penelope to dance, and as he led her away, Daniel turned to Miss Chartfield.

"You seem to have a great many cousins," he observed. She was wearing a sophisticated gown of sapphire silk, a dazzling diamond and sapphire necklace clasped about her throat. He thought she looked quite elegant, although he could not help but think her polished perfection suffered in comparrison to Penelope's more natural beauty.

"I have a great many aunts and uncles," she replied, laughing as she unfurled her fan with practiced grace. "You must apply to them if you find fault with the quantity of their offspring."

"I did not mean to imply fault," he hastened to assure her. "I was merely making an observation. But speaking of your cousins, where is Mr. Bellamy? Will he be joining us tonight?"

"He will be here a little later," Miss Chartfield answered, a slight frown puckering her brows. "He was supposed to ride with us, but at the last moment he sent a note saying he'd been detained and to go on without him."

Daniel murmured something appropriate, although he was secretly relieved at being spared the other man's company. Haworth's sycophancy had already turned his stomach, and he did not think he could tolerate another fawning popinjay dripping flattery all over him.

"I was surprised not to see you or your sister at the Academy today, Mr. Grantham," Miss Chartfield said, her blue eyes studying him over the edge of her fan. "There was a lecture on the ruins of Crete. Have you no interest in antiquities?"

The remark made Daniel remember the lecture he'd been planning to attend since learning of it, and he swallowed an impatient oath. "Indeed, I have," he said, thinking of the disappointing day he'd spent laying plans with Polson. "Unfortunately I had a previous engagement. How was it?"

She quickly related the details of the lecture, making him chuckle as she described how her cousin the captain blushed every time the lecturer displayed his drawings of the scantily attired statues. "I shudder to think how Horatio will respond should he have cause to examine Lord Townley's marbles," she said, her lips curving in a rueful smile. "Miss Reynolds assures me they are even more shocking than those Mr. Goodkin described."

"Then I should suggest, ma'am, that you take care to spare your poor cousin's delicate sensibilities," Daniel said, flicking an amused glance in the captain's direction. He and Penelope were still on the dance floor, and if her wooden expression was any indication, she was finding the experience less than pleasant. As if sensing his thoughts she lifted her head and met his gaze, her nose wrinkling in a gamine grimace.

"I shall try to keep that in mind," Miss Chartfield said, and something in the inflection of her voice brought Daniel's attention snapping back to her. She looked decidedly troubled, and he reached out to cover her hand with his own.

"Is something wrong?" he asked, his tone gentle as he studied her face. "You look as if something is vexing you."

"Not vexing, precisely," she said, raising her gaze to meet his. "But there is something I wish to ask you, and I can not think how to do it without giving offense."

Daniel felt a *frisson* of fear, wondering what he would do if she began pressing him for information he dared not provide. "The only way to do it is to simply ask," he said, striving to sound no more than intrigued. "But I promise to do my best not to fly up into the boughs. What is it you wish to know?"

She hesitated a moment as if marshalling her courage. "I hope you will not take this amiss," she said, her voice sounding slightly breathless, "but as we were coming through the door, I happened to notice you were conversing with Lord Haworth."

"We were introduced this evening by Lord Burlington," he responded, his shoulders slumping with unconscious relief.

"And if you are about to tell me his lordship is not all he should be, you need not bother. My mother made mention of the fact as we were arriving."

Miss Chartfield's cheeks grew as rosy as her cousin's. "This is going to make me sound dreadfully high in the instep," she said, her lashes lowering in embarrassment, "but as you are new to London I did not know if you knew of the marquess's . . . er . . ."

"Dubious reputation?" Daniel concluded, taking pity on her pretty distress. He knew she wasn't so much snobbish as she was concerned, and he gathered she had felt duty-bound to warn him and Penelope off before their names were linked with Haworth's. He appreciated the effort, and it made him wonder if she might be able to shed further light on some of the gossip Mrs. Grantham had let slip in the carriage.

"Come now, Miss Chartfield, surely Lord Haworth's name can not be so black as all that," he added, tilting his head to one side and offering her a beguiling smile. "If it were, I am sure the Fitzroys should never have admitted him in their home, and certainly the viscount would not have introduced him to us if the mere act of being seen in his company placed us beyond the pale."

"Would he not?" she said waspishly, and then looked contrite. "I am sorry, Mr. Grantham. I know we have pulled caps over his lordship before, but the plain truth is Lord Burlington is little better than his friend. My aunt Louisa says he is young and so one must forgive him his foibles, but it seems as if he is going from bad to worse. And I had such hopes for—" she broke off, a look of utter horror spreading across her face.

Her words as well as her telling expression intrigued Daniel, and he didn't hesitate pressing her for further information. "Pray continue, Miss Chartfield," he said, assuming a somber mein. "You may rely upon my complete discretion, I assure you."

She hesitated, her teeth worrying her bottom lip before she gave a troubled sigh. "I met his lordship at a house party two years ago," she began, casting him an apprehensive look, "and he struck me as a care-for-nothing dandy more interested in ladybirds than in making anything of himself. Then his brother died, and it was as if he aged overnight.''

"Perhaps he was merely mourning his brother," Daniel suggested, careful not to reveal too much. "It is not unusual for a man to change after suffering so sad a loss."

"Yes, but it was more than that," Miss Chartfield said, gesturing impatiently. "Admittedly Lord Burlington and I are not well-acquainted, but even I could not help but mark the difference in his behavior. He became more serious, his actions more deliberate. I thought it meant he was growing up at long last, but then he began associating with Lord Haworth, and now I do not know what to think."

Daniel digested what he had learned in silence. Polson had already told him Haworth had been currying Andrew's favor, but that Andrew had rebuffed him . . . until recently.

He turned his head, his gaze searching the crowded ballroom until he spied Andrew standing by the French doors leading out on to the balcony. He was alone, his own gaze fixed on Haworth, who was a few feet away, and the cold, determined expression on his brother's face made Daniel frown.

"Mr. Grantham?" The touch of Miss Chartfield's hand on his sleeve brought Daniel's attention back to her, and he reluctantly tore his gaze from Andrew to look down in her face.

"I hope I have not given you a horror of me," she said, gazing up at him shyly. "I am not usually so priggish, I promise you. It is just I hate to see a man squander his life as the viscount is squandering his."

Daniel covered her hand with his own for a brief moment. "I understand, ma'am," he said, suddenly anxious to be alone. His head was spinning with a dozen different thoughts and emotions, and he desired nothing more than a few minutes peace so that he could sort through them.

"That is very good of you, sir, " Miss Chartfield replied, lowering her lashes demurely. "I should hate to think you regard me as one of those tiresome females who are forever finding fault with others."

"Never ma'am," he assured her, his lips lifting in a genuine smile. And it was the truth, he realized, feeling vaguely surprised. How could he dislike Miss Chartfield's actions when they reminded him of something Penelope would do under similar circumstances? Except, he admitted, his eyes gleaming with silent laughter, she would die sooner than uttering anything even remotely resembling an apology.

Miss Chartfield took a step back from him, evidently deciding she had lingered in his company long enough. "If you will forgive me, I can see my cousin, Mr. Bellamy, has arrived, and I mean to go read him a scold," she said, her voice overly bright. "Pray give my best to your mother and sister." She scurried away as fast as decorum would allow.

Lord, would tonight never end? Penelope wondered morosely, her face stiff from the effort of keeping her foolish smile in place. She had danced with several young men, each more clumsy than the last, and her temper as well as her feet had endured all they could. If just one more tiresome puppy asked her to dance, she vowed, she would toss him into the orgeat bowl.

"Good evening, Miss Grantham." The deep voice of Lord Burlington jolted her out of her brown study, and she glanced up to find him standing beside her.

"My lord." She dropped a hasty curtsey, not so lost to the proprieties as to commit mayhem upon a viscount.

"It seems as if you are enjoying a pleasant evening," his lordship said, his eyes studying her intently. "May I hope you have this dance free so that I may partner you?"

Despite her earlier thoughts, Penelope managed to drag up a polite smile. "That would be very nice, my lord, thank you," she said, praying he was as light on his feet as he looked. She did not think her poor toes would withstand another assault.

"I noticed your brother speaking with Miss Chartfield," Lord Burlington said, his hand firm on her elbow as he guided her to the dance floor, were couples were assembling for the next set.

"Yes, he and Miss Chartfield share an interest in science," Penelope said, hoping the dance wasn't a quadrille. She had the worst time keeping the steps in their proper order.

"Do they?" The viscount's eyebrow lifted in haughty inquiry. "How interesting. But then, I have been hearing much of your brother and his talent for science. I am sorry we haven't met sooner. It is rather embarrassing to have such a renowned scientist in one's own neighborhood and not be aware of it."

Something in his cool observation made Penelope glance up at him in surprise. "You know what they say, my lord," she said, wondering why the words had sounded so familiar to her. " 'No man is a prophet in his own kingdom.' "

The viscount's lips formed a smile that did not quite reach his eyes. "An astute observation, Miss Grantham. It would seem intellectual ability is something of a family trait."

The opening strains of a country dance relieved Penelope of the necessity of a reply, and she spent the next several minutes concentrating on the intricate dance steps. But even as she was doing her best not to put her foot wrong, she was brooding over the viscount and his odd behavior.

She was certain he had asked her to dance for some reason other than mere politeness, and she wondered what that reason might be. She also wondered what there was about him that had her senses jangling in alarm. The sensation reminded her of how she felt when conducting an experiment that was about to go wrong. She sensed she had forgotten something vital, but for the life of her, she could not think what that something might be.

The dance soon ended, and other than stepping on the train of the lady's gown beside her, Penelope felt she gave a good accounting of herself. The viscount escorted her back to the corner, but any hopes she might have harbored that he would leave her in peace were dashed when he offered to escort her to the refreshment table. As she had no idea how to politely refuse his charming request, she gave in with what she hoped was a proper show of enthusiasm.

"I have been meaning to ask you, ma'am, how long you and your family have lived in Bibury," his lordship said as he guided her into the elegant salon where Lady Fitzroy had set up a table loaded with sweets and other tempting delicacies. "I recall when Squire Davison, who originally owned your house, died, but I fear I can not remember when you and your family moved in.''

''It was approximately four years ago,'' Penelope said, accepting the cup of champagne punch a footman offered her.

''Ah yes, that would be about right. And prior to that, where did you reside?''

''We are originally from Shropshire, a small village not far from the Welsh border,'' Penelope replied, her wariness increasing. ''My grandfather was a successful merchant in Shrewsbury, and he had a manor house built in the country.''

''I thought I detected a hint of a lyrical quality to your voice.'' The viscount gave her another of his ice-edged smiles. ''Have you any Welsh in your blood, Miss Grantham?''

''My mother's grandmother was of Welsh extraction, but I fear I haven't an ounce of musical ability. My brother, however, has a lovely singing voice,'' Penelope replied, wondering what he was hinting at. She was certain his questions were far from arbitrary, although what he was hinting at, she knew not.

''Does he?'' Lord Burlington drawled, and something in the inflection of his deep voice put her strongly in mind of Daniel.

That was what was troubling her, she realized with a shock. Lord Burlington's resemblance to Daniel was more marked than ever, and stealing a glance at his face, Penelope found herself wondering again if Daniel's connection to the viscount's family was as remote as he claimed.

Daniel's eyes were a darker green, and his thick hair was a darker shade as well. He was taller and more muscular than Lord Burlington, but she thought that might be because his lordship was still a relatively young man. But it was as she studied the viscount's face that the resemblance became more pronounced.

Their noses had the same aquiline construction, she decided, forcing herself to observe the matter objectively, and the shape of their lips was startlingly similar. Even the way Lord Burlington moved and the way he spoke reminded her of Daniel, and she wondered how she could have been so foolish as not to tumble to the truth at once. It also made her realize the viscount was equally aware of the resemblance, and she knew now what he was trying to discern. He was trying to learn if

Daniel might be related to him in some fashion.

"Of course," she said, speaking rapidly to hide her confusion, "my father was famous for his singing voice as well, and that is doubtlessly where Ulysses came by his talent. Papa served as choir master for our village church when I was younger."

His lordship's expression remained unchanged. "I recall hearing he died some two years ago," he said, his manner as coolly relentless as Daniel's. "I am sorry to hear that. My own father died when I was scarce out of my teens, and I lost both my brothers within a year of each other."

Penelope softened at the pain she detected in his voice. The poor man had lost his entire family in a very short span of time, so perhaps he couldn't be blamed for his ruthless quest. If she lost her family, she supposed she would also want to find any remaining relation, however tenuous the connection might be. Still, she did not think it wise to reveal Daniel's true identity just yet. Not until after the presentation before the Royal Society.

"I was wondering, Miss Grantham, if I might call upon you and your brother tomorrow," Lord Burlington said, his ever-watchful gaze fastened to her face. "It occurs to me that it is past time I offered your brother my patronage, and I should like to discuss the matter with him."

Penelope's plate of cakes and lobster patties wobbled wildly in her hands, but she managed not to drop it. "I . . . that is very kind of you, my lord," she stammered, trying to think of what she should do. "I shall certainly mention the matter to my brother."

"Then I may call upon you?"

"Yes—no!" Belatedly she remembered the visit to the Royal Society's laboratory Daniel had promised her. "That is to say," she corrected when she saw his eyebrows arch in haughty inquiry, "you may certainly call upon us, but I fear tomorrow is not convenient. Another day, perhaps?"

"That is very kind of you, Miss Grantham, thank you," he said, accepting her offer with a cool nod. "I shall send a footman with a message, and we shall set up a time acceptable to us both. In the meanwhile I fear I must take my leave of you.

Haworth and I are promised at another party. Good night, ma'am." He gave her another bow and walked away, leaving her to stew in her own troubling thoughts.

She finished the food on her plate and returned to the ballroom to search for Daniel. She didn't see him at first, but then a movement near the French doors caught her eye and she saw him walking in from the balcony. She picked up the skirts of her dress and rushed to his side.

"We have to talk," she said, her voice breathless as she gazed up at him. "Alone."

His eyebrow lifted at the last word. "Of course, sister," he said, inclining his head in the direction of the balcony. "Would you care for a breath of fresh air?"

She followed him silently, and the moment they were alone she turned to face him. "I just spoke with Lord Burlington," she said, getting to the heart of the matter at once. "He is offering to stand as your sponsor."

Daniel leaned back against the stone balustrade and folded his arms across his chest. "Is he?" he asked, his voice lacking any inflection. "Did he say why he was being so generous?"

Penelope was uncertain how to reply. What she knew and what she suspected were two different things, and she vacillated between the two before giving a dispirited sigh. "I think he suspects you are related to him," she said at last.

Daniel's arms dropped to his side. "What did you say?"

Penelope related the details of her odd conversation with the viscount. She tried to be as concise as possible, keeping her interpretations clearly separate from her observations. When she finished, Daniel looked as if he had been struck by an unprotected charge of electricity.

"He thinks I am his brother?" he repeated, his usually deep voice going up several octaves. "My God, are you certain?"

"No, I am not certain," she admitted, determined to be as honest as she could. "But that is what I *think* he believes. His questions were far too pointed to be mere coincidence, and then there is the fact the two of you are as alike as two peas in a pod." She gave him a considering look. "Are you quite certain the relationship between you is no closer than distant cousins?"

He flinched as if she had struck him, and even in the faint light filtering out from the ballroom she could see he had paled. "What do you mean by that?" he demanded, his voice low with fury.

There were times when discretion was appropriate, and times when it was not. And this, Penelope decided resolutely, was definitely one of the latter. She raised her chin, as she met Daniel's stormy gaze.

"I mean, sir, that I am weary of the evasions and half-truths you have been giving whenever I ask about your past," she said bluntly. "There is too much at stake for prevarication, and I want an honest answer. Is there a possibility, however small, that you could be the viscount's brother?"

There was a heavy pause, and Penelope thought he was going to refuse to answer. He looked so hard; so cold and unwavering, he might have been carved from marble. Then inexplicably his shoulders drooped, and he squeezed his eyes shut.

"Penelope," he began hollowly, and she reached up to lay a gentle finger against his lips.

"No, Daniel," she said, perilously close to tears. "Just the truth. I know I've given you little cause to trust me, but—"

He jerked his head back in shock, his hand flying up to capture hers in a fierce grip. "Of course I trust you!" he snapped, his eyes glittering as he scowled down at her. "How can you think I do not?"

Penelope gaped up at him. "I—I have been less than ethical," she stammered, trying to ignore the affect his nearness was having on her good senses. "The first time I clapped eyes on you I offered you money to pose as Ulysses. Given that, I can hardly blame you if you had some concerns about my veracity."

His hands slid across her shoulders until she was trapped between his warm palms. "What utter rot!" he announced, his scowl growing more marked. "You're the most honest woman I know. I should trust you with my life."

"Then why won't you tell me the truth?" she cried, propriety forgotten as she cupped his face in her hands. "You *are* Lord Burlington's brother, aren't you?'' He didn't reply. ''Aren't you?''

His jaw clenched beneath her fingers, the muscle so tight, she thought it would snap. His eyes took on a wild glitter, and then all light in them died out as he gave a heavy sigh.

''Yes. Yes, I am.''

10

Daniel stepped back from Penelope, his heart clenching at the stunned look on her face. He had been seeing that look in his dreams ever since he began toying with the idea of telling her the truth. At first he'd hoped such honesty wouldn't prove necessary, and then, coward that he was, he'd hoped to wait until the last moment before apprising her of the situation. Now, when he was least prepared for it, the truth in all of its ugliness had exploded in his face. 'Twould seem the poets were right, he thought with a flash of gallows humor; truth will out.

"Why did you not say so before now?" she asked, and he could see the hurt tears shimmering in the golden-green depths of her eyes. "Was it because you are ill—illegitimate?" She stumbled over the hateful word, her pale cheeks suffusing with color.

He hesitated, tempted almost beyond endurance to grasp at the most logical explanation. If she thought him a bastard, he knew she could be trusted to keep silent about his birth. But when he saw the compassion shinning from her, he knew he couldn't repay her kindness with more lies.

"No," he said at last, his voice rough from his emotions. "It is because it was easier that way. Things are . . . complicated," he concluded, and then gave a weak laugh at how inadequately that word described the tangle of his life.

"How is it complicated?" Penelope pressed, determined to understand what he was saying. "Has it anything to do with your father?" she added, her brows gathering in a frown. "Did he know of your existence but refuse to acknowledge you?"

He knew she was still thinking him his father's by-blow, and shook his head. "Oh, he knew of my existence, all right," he said, unable to hold back the old bitterness. "As for refusing to acknowledge me, he did that in the cruelest way you can imagine. He told everyone I was dead, and even put up a marker in my memory. I was studying it a few minutes before we met."

"A marker?" Her expression grew more perplexed, and he could see she was trying to picture the old graveyard. Suddenly her eye flew wide, and she gazed up at him in horrified disbelief. "But—but that would make you . . ."

"Daniel Warfield," he finished for her, his lips stretching into a grim smile. "I know."

"But Daniel Warfield was lost at sea," she said at last, her voice weak. "I heard the story when I first came to Bibury. There was a storm, and the ship went down with all hands."

"That is what father wanted the world to think," Daniel said, anger and a hurt he had refused to face making him feel almost ill. "It seems he preferred a dead son to one who defied him the way I did."

"But that is infamous!" Penelope cried, the fire returning to her eyes. "How could a father do that to his own son?"

He found her outrage on his behalf oddly touching, and because of that he was willing to give his father his due. "To be fair, he was not totally without cause." His lips curved as he recalled the wild youth he had been. "I was a hellion without equal in those days. I drank, consorted with lightskirts, and squandered as much money as I could manage. He bailed me out of one scrape out of another, until he'd finally had enough."

"And then he banished you to America and declared you dead?" she interrupted, clearly scandalized. "He sounds the vilest monster to ever draw breath!"

Daniel was astonished to find himself defending his father. "Not quite," he corrected. "Family tradition dictated the third son go into the church, and after the last fiasco he told me he was done with pulling me out of the suds. He controlled the living at a small parish outside of Lancaster, and he informed me I was to go there once I finished my schooling.''

"And you refused?''

Daniel's smile widened at her question. "I was twenty years old and no more interested in becoming a rector than I was in flying to the moon," he said wryly. "A friend of mine, Geoffrey Canton, was from America, and we often talked of my visiting him and his family. I had it in mind to spend a year or so with him exploring the country, and when I suggested this to my father, he refused to even discuss it.''

"And the more he refused to discuss it, the more set you became on making the journey?" Penelope guessed, and then nodded her head. "Yes, I can see your reacting like that.''

"You are too kind," Daniel drawled, amused by her ready acceptance of his defiant behavior. "As I say, I was twenty years old, and there is no one on the face of this earth who knows more than a twenty year old—especially a twenty year old as pampered and headstrong as I was. I was convinced my father was in the wrong, and when he threatened to consider me dead if I set sail, I snapped my fingers at him. *That* is what I thought of his rules, I told him, and I left.''

"And you never came home?" Penelope asked after a thoughtful pause. "You never wrote in all those years you were gone?''

"Father made it clear that if I left, letters from me would be returned unopened," he answered, feeling anew the bitter pain of his father's rejection. "And in those first five years I was still too angry and belligerent to put pen to paper, even when I was in an agony of homesickness. After that . . .'' He gave an uncomfortable shrug. "I don't know, I suppose I thought it best. What is done can not be undone, and all that. I'd made a life for myself in Charleston, a good one; and I could see no point in coming home to face the old anger and recriminations.''

"Then you are from Charleston?" she asked, studying his face speculatively. "I'll admit I was beginning to wonder.''

Her suspicion stung, even as he understood the reasons for

it. "I own a town house in Charleston and a smaller plantation in the low country, near Beaufort," he said, and then raised his chin proudly. "Also, I truly am an American citizen. I didn't lie about that."

"And Canton is your friend's name?" she asked, ignoring the last part of his reply.

"Yes," he said, his heart warming at the thought of his closest friend. "Geoffrey Canton. We were at Eaton together and later we shared rooms at Oxford. He is a most remarkable fellow," he added, smiling at Penelope. "He has a passion for science and learning, and there is nothing he likes better than burying his nose in some dusty book. You'd like him, I think."

"I am sure I would," she answered with a sniff, "but we were discussing you. Why did you come back to England after all these years? You must have had some reason."

The light-heartedness he'd begun feeling died at her blunt question. "Oh, I did," he assured her softly. "I learned my parents were dead, and that there was no way I could ever make peace with my father. I realized then I'd wasted enough time in foolish defiance, and I decided it was time to return home. I was making arrangements to leave when word reached me that my brother, Richard, and my other brother, James, had died within months of each other."

Penelope's expression softened, and she laid a gentle hand on his arm. "I am so sorry, Daniel," she said, her gaze lambent. "I know how much that must have hurt you. There are times when I feel like throttling Ulysses, but I can't imagine what it would be like to lose him."

"There's more," he said, his voice strained as he covered her hand with his own. "Shortly after my return I discovered there was some mystery about their deaths, especially Richard's, and I knew I would not rest until I had the truth."

Penelope digested that in silence. "The marquess?" she asked, alluding to her mother's earlier remarks in the carriage.

Daniel nodded. "He was there both times when my brothers died, and I have since learned he had reasons to wish Richard ill. He was the most likely place to start, and I knew if I hoped to discover anything I would have to meet him. Unfortunately, my father's machinations made that impossible."

"Because he had declared you dead, you mean?" Penelope asked. "Yes, I can see where being mistaken for a corpse would prove slightly disaccommodating, but couldn't you have just come forward and told everyone there had been a mistake?"

He sighed and gave her an impatient look. "Penelope, with Richard and James dead, I am next in line to the title. Think how it would look if I appeared out of nowhere just as I stood to inherit a fortune. Rather convenient, do you not agree?"

Her jaw dropped as understanding dawned. "My heavens, are you saying they would suspect *you*?" she gasped in horror. "But that is ridiculous! You would never do such a thing!"

"You are saying that only because you know me," he reminded her. "But if you did not know me, you have to admit it is a theory that makes more than a bit of sense. Who better than the dissolute third son to eliminate those who stood between him and a title? Certainly it makes better sense than to lay the blame on a marquess, however muddied his reputation."

He could tell by her expression that she saw the logic of what he said, and was horrified by it. "When you repeated your offer to me to pose as Ulysses, I realized I was being offered the perfect opportunity to investigate Haworth," he said, determined to hold nothing back. "That was why I agreed. I saw you as a tool to be used; nothing else."

Penelope started to answer and then stopped, her glance suddenly going over his shoulder. He turned just as another couple walked out on to the balcony. They stopped at the sight of Penelope and him standing there, and the man offered them a mocking bow.

"Beg pardon, old boy," he told Daniel, his voice slurred with drink. "Didn't know you and your light o'love were out here. Don't mind sharing the moonlight, I trust?"

Daniel stiffened in fury, pushing Penelope behind him as he took a menacing step forward. "You mistake the matter, sir," he said, his voice coldly cutting. "The lady is my sister, and you will apologize for your insult."

"Sister?" The man's fleshy lips twisted in a sneer. "You

don't expect me to believe that old saw, do you?''

Daniel grabbed the other man by his labels, ignoring his paramour's shriek as he jerked him off his feet. "I *expect* that you will either apologize or name your seconds," he said, giving the man a vicious shake for emphasis. "Which is it to be?"

The man's florid face paled, and he cast Penelope a desperate look. "Beg your pardon, ma'am," he said, his voice shaking with fear. "No disrespect meant, 'pon my rep!"

Daniel released him, making no attempt to hide his contempt as he flung the man against the side of the balcony. "You had best pray I never learn your name," he advised him, his hands clenching and unclenching as he took a step back. "If I do, or if I learn you have wagged your vicious tongue unwisely, I may decide your apology is not quite enough. Is that understood?"

The other man nodded rapidly, grabbing his companion's hand and inching back from Daniel. "Indeed, sir, clear as ice. Good night to you, ma'am," he said, and stumbled through the billowing drapes.

Daniel stared after him before turning back to Penelope. "We have been out here rather a long time," he said in a strained voice. "Perhaps it would be best if we rejoined the others."

She blinked at him. "But Daniel—"

"No." He firmly shook his head. "I have said all I intend to say for the moment. We can talk later if you wish, but for now I think we should return to the ballroom. Come." He offered her his arm, leaving her no choice but to acquiesce.

She glared at him for several seconds and then gave a loud sigh. "Oh, very well, you tyrant," she grumbled, moving forward to take his arm. "But if you think this is the end of it, you may think again. I have several questions, and I shan't rest until I have asked them."

He cast her a quick glance out of the corner of his eyes, his heart sinking at the belligerent set of her jaw. "Of that, Miss Grantham, I have no doubt," he said with a sigh. "I only hope I shall have the answers."

* * *

Penelope spent a restless night grappling with her conscience and her heart. Daniel's revelation had stunned her, and even as she acknowledged he'd had no other choice but to act as he had, there was a part of her that was deeply hurt at what she viewed as his deception.

It wasn't as if she would have blabbed the truth to anyone who would have listened, she thought sourly, shifting onto her back to glare up at the ceiling. Indeed, given the nature of the fraud *she* was committing upon society, how could he have thought her so eager to spill his secrets? He may have stood to be accused of murder, but she would have been faced with social ruination were her dark secret revealed. It was said there was no honor among thieves, and now it appeared there was little trust to be found amongst fellow conspirators!

Even as this uncharitable thought formed, she chastised herself for it. Daniel was no thief, and he could hardly be faulted by choosing not to confess his identity to someone who was a virtual stranger. Further, his reasons for posing as Ulysses were far less self-serving than her own. She had only been interested in selfish glory, while he had been pursuing a murderer. If she thought someone guilty of killing her brother, she would have gone after them with everything she had, and may the Devil take the hindmost!

Thinking of Daniel's reasons for his deception was preferable to brooding over his failure to confide in her, and she decided to give that her full attention. A plan was clearly necessary if the marquess was to be caught, and she whiled away the hours reviewing various possibilities before drifting into sleep.

The maid bringing her a cup of chocolate roused her late the next morning, and she rose bleary-eyed to face her day. As Daniel hadn't sent a note crying off from going to the laboratory she surmised the visit was still on, and dressed accordingly in one of her oldest, plainest gowns.

"Are you certain that is what you wish to wear?" her abigail queried, a pained expression on her face. "It is rather . . . er . . . drab," she concluded, fluttering her hands in weak disapproval.

"I am going to a laboratory, Annette, not the court at St.

James,'' Penelope replied, eyeing the simple gray merino dress with an odd sense of dissatisfaction. After so many weeks of dressing to the nines she had become accustomed to silks and lace, and the dress, which had always been one of her favorites, now felt as if it belonged to someone else. She wondered what Daniel would think to see her dressed so plainly, and gave a horrified start.

It was just as well the demonstration was almost upon them, she decided, turning away from the glass with a shudder. If she remained in London another month, she would doubtlessly be as slavishly devoted to fashion as the greenest deb.

''Fetch the apron from my clothes press, Annette, and I shall be on my way,'' she said, her voice cool to hide her dismay.

''An apron?'' Annette's eyes widened in almost comical horror. ''But Miss Grantham, you can not wear an apron with that . . . that dress! People will take you for a maid!''

''Let them,'' Penelope replied with a shrug, refusing to allow her maid's protest to detour her. ''I shall be wearing a cloak while we're on the street, so you needn't fear anyone shall lay the blame for my lack of elegance on your doorstep. Not unless I tell them, that is,'' she added, sliding a meaningful glance in the maid's direction that had her scurrying to retrieve the requested apron.

Fashioned from strong sailcloth, the apron was even more hideous than her gown, but it protected her from any spills or splatters from the corrosive chemicals she often handled, and that far outweighed its ugliness in Penelope's mind. A pair of gloves made from the same material were tucked in the apron's pocket, and after making sure they were still there, she hurried downstairs to find Daniel waiting for her. His drawn face showed he had slept as poorly as she had, and she wasn't surprised when he suggested that they take a carriage rather than walking as they had previously done.

''I know you are brimming with questions,'' he said the moment the coach pulled away from the house, ''but I must ask that you hold them for now. The demonstration is but a sennight away, and there is much I still must learn if we are ever to pull this thing off. Do you agree?''

She did not, but he looked so haggard she could not find it in her to argue the matter. Besides, she reminded herself with a tiny sigh, given his size and stubbornness she could hardly force secrets from him he was determined not to give. "As you say, Daniel," she said, inclining her head with what she thought great dignity. "Is there anything you have learned that you don't understand? If so, I should be happy to explain it to you."

He shot a look of disbelief at her compliance, but then began discussing a few questions which had apparently been troubling him. By the time the carriage clattered to a halt in front of the Royal Society, Penelope had managed to put the mystery surrounding the deaths of Daniel's brother from her mind.

The laboratories were located in the Society's basement, and a quick glance had Penelope turning an unbecoming shade of green. "Leyden jars," she sighed, gazing up at the shelves of glass receptacles. "Rows and rows of Leyden jars. No wonder I have difficulty obtaining any; these wretches are hogging them all."

Daniel's lips quirked in a smile as he joined her. "What the devil are Leyden jars?" he asked curiously.

She reached up and retrieved one of the foil-coated jars. "They are used as an electrical condenser," she said, carefully removing the insulated stopper. "As you can see they are lined with a metallic layer, which connects with the conducting rod."

He ducked his dark head, his hair brushing against her arm as he picked up the thin rod. "I see," he said, sounding genuinely intrigued by the device. "How does it figure in your work?"

"It stores electrical charges so that I can study and measure them," she replied, her nose twitching as the fragrance of pine, underlayed with a warm spice, wafted up from Daniel's freshly shaven cheeks. She'd smelled his cologne before, but she couldn't recall the odor making her feel light-headed. It must be her excitement at being in the laboratory, but she shifted to one side so Daniel's body was no longer brushing against her own.

"What then?" he asked, handing her back the jar. "I understand your theory about there being both negative and positive properties to electricity, but I still do not understand how they relate to magnetism."

"I believe electricity and magnetism are connected," Penelope replied, elated at discussing her work with a man who paid such rapt attention. "And if electricity can be both negative and positive, it is logical to assume magnetism would follow suit. The experiment I am proposing to conduct will expose a compass—which as we know has magnetic properties—to an electrified wire. If the needle of the compass moves in correspondence to the wire, it will prove the relationship exists."

"*If* it moves?" he repeated, his brow arching. "Do you mean you do not know? Haven't you conducted this experiment yet?"

She bit her lip. "Yes, but the results weren't quite what I had hoped for. The needle did move, but not in the direction I was expecting. Instead of moving with the electrical current it moved at a right angle, and it did so consistently, so I know it wasn't an accident. I think the current produces some sort of force which circles around the wire, causing the effect."

Daniel looked perplexed. "Why is that, do you think?"

"I don't know," she admitted, wrinkling her nose at him. "I think it is because the wire itself somehow became magnetized by its proximity to the compass, and the effect was a result of the interaction between the two magnets, but I'm not certain. Of course," she added, tilting her head as a sudden thought occurred to her, "that doesn't explain how the magnetism process itself occurred, but perhaps that is something that will become clearer with further experimentation."

"Mmm." Daniel stroked his jaw. "And this is the experiment you propose I perform in front of the society?"

"Yes; it is the one that drew the most interest."

"Then we had best get started," he sighed, his fingers nimbly unfastening the buttons on his coat of Bath superfine. "We shall be at this all day if I don't wish to make a complete fool of myself in front of all London."

One of the laboratory helpers, whose job it was to wash the

jars and other instruments, found an old coat and apron which he politely offered Daniel. In deference to the hard work and the muggy atmosphere Daniel also shed his cravat, and Penelope was treated to a glimpse of his tanned throat before she became caught up in the intricacies of the experiment.

To her delight Daniel proved a most apt pupil, and even if he became a trifle impatient with himself at times, she began to actually believe they would succeed. Although she would have died sooner than admit it, she was beginning to have some serious trepidations. When he conducted the experiment successfully with only a little prompting from her, she gave a triumphant crow of laughter.

"You did it!" she cried, flinging her arms about his neck and planting an excited kiss on his cheek. "Oh, Daniel, you did it!"

"Of course I did," he responded, his arms closing about her waist and lifting her off the floor. "Did you think I could not, with such a taskmaster driving me?"

"Taskmaster?" she protested, a laugh bubbling up from her throat as he swung her about in a circle. "How dare you call me that, you wretch! Put me down this moment!"

In response he gave a merry laugh and whirled her around again. "And if I don't?" he teased, lifting her higher so that she was gazing down into his eyes. "What will you do then, my sweet tyrant, hm?"

Penelope started to answer, but the sight of his mouth, inches from her own, drove the words from her mind. She stared down at his lips, her insides going soft and warm as she wondered what it would be like to feel them against her own. Her hands clenched on his muscular shoulders, her eyes fluttering closed as a soft sigh escaped her lips.

She could feel his muscles tense, and then he slowly lowered her until she could feel the warmth of his breath feathering against her lips. She heard a low groan, and then his mouth covered hers in a kiss that drove any thoughts of protest from her mind.

His mouth was ardent as it brushed against hers, the movements both commanding and pleading as they drew a response from deep inside her. He tasted so sweet, so enticing, that she wanted even more. When he increased the pressure of his lips, she parted her own, and was rewarded when he deepened the kiss with a mastery that made her sigh.

"Penelope," he moaned, his arms locking her close. "Kiss me, my darling. Kiss me the way I am kissing you."

His plea filled her with a deep, feminine excitement and she shyly did as he asked, revelling in the hot taste of his mouth. Her heart was racing in unison with the heart she could feel pounding against her breasts, and the sensation made her ache. Daniel's kiss was everything she had ever dreamed a kiss could be, and even as she told herself she should draw back, she longed for even greater intimacies.

Her hands slid into the midnight depths of his hair, her fingertips lightly caressing the back of his neck. She could feel the strength in him, contrasting sharply with the warm sensuality he was showing her. She knew he could overwhelm any resistance she might make, and the knowledge he would not gave her a heady sense of freedom. She flicked her tongue teasingly against his and heard a tortured moan catch in his throat.

Daniel drew back, his breath coming unevenly from between his teeth as his burning gaze met hers. His eyes were almost pure emerald with desire, and the look in them filled her with sudden desolation. There was more than passion shining in the jewel-colored depths, there was regret as well, and it was all she could do not to cry out at the agony consuming her.

"Penelope . . ." She could hear the contrition in his voice, and knew it would kill her if he apologized. Dragging the remnants of her pride about her, she managed a ferocious scowl and administered a playful swat to his shoulder.

"Is this how you treat poor innocent females you find in laboratories?" she scolded, hiding her pain behind a teasing facade. "If so, you are an even bigger rogue than that villain Haworth. Now set me down this instant, before I tell Mama."

He hesitated, and for a moment she feared he was going to apologize anyway. Then he slowly set her down, his hands lingering briefly on her waist before he stepped away from her. "If I am a rogue, it was not without some enticement, you heartless wench," he responded, flicking his finger down the front of her soiled apron. "How else is a man to respond when presented with such elegance and beauty?"

"Brat." She batted his hand away, scowling and rearranging her hair in an tidy bundle at the nape of her neck. It had come undone at some point, and it took several seconds to restore it to any semblance of order.

While she attended to her *toilet* he retied his cravat and put on his jacket, and by the time she was finished, he was waiting for her by the door. By unspoken agreement they decided to walk home, and were soon making their way down Picadilly. The street was as busy as ever, and they were stepping around a crowd of young bloods clustered around a bow window when a familiar voice called out to them.

"Mr. Grantham, Miss Grantham, wait!"

They turned, and saw Miss Reynolds scurrying towards them, Mr. Bellamy hot on her heels.

"Thank heaven I have found you!" she exclaimed, her cheeks flushed with exertion. "I am in the most dire straits, Miss Grantham, and I am praying that you will rescue me!"

Penelope exchanged a bemused look with Daniel. "I shall certainly be willing to try, Miss Reynolds. What seems to be the problem?" she asked, forcing herself to sound civil. She was still reeling from the kiss she and Daniel exchanged, and the last thing she wanted was to deal with Miss Reynolds in one of her flighty moods. Despite the other woman's scientific interests, Penelope had concluded she was the greatest peagoose she had ever met.

"I am on my way to a meeting of the Ladies Society for Scientific Advancement," Miss Reynolds continued breathlessly, "and I just remembered I was to provide the speaker. I had intended asking you all along, of course, but it slipped my mind, and now I find myself at *point non plus*. If you do not agree to speak I shall be quite, quite ruined."

The idea of spending an entire afternoon in the other woman's company was not at all to Penelope's liking, and she tried to think of some graceful way to extract herself from the situation. "I should be honored to address your group," she said, seizing the first excuse she could think of. "Unfortunately I promised my mother I would come straight home, and—''

"Why don't you go with her, Penelope?" Daniel interrupted, turning to her with a strained smile. "I shall tell Mama where you are going, if you would like. I am sure she shan't mind."

"Oh, but you must come as well, Mr. Grantham!" Miss Reynolds implored, turning her gray-blue eyes in his direction. "Our Society is open to men as well, and we should be delighted to have such a noted scientist honor us with his presence."

Penelope knew a moment of sadistic glee that Daniel had been hoisted with his own petard, and she hastened to speak before he could cry off. "What an excellent idea, Miss Reynolds!" she gushed, laying her hand on Daniel's arm to keep him from bolting. "We'd be delighted to accompany you, wouldn't we, Ulysses?" She cast him a simpering smile, her eyes gleaming with triumph.

His lips twitched, but he did not smile. "As you wish," he drawled, the look in his deep-green eyes promising revenge before he turned to Miss Reynolds and Mr. Bellamy. "My sister and I shall be happy to accompany you, ma'am," he told her, his manner as smoothly polished as marble. "Where is the meeting to be held, if I may ask?"

"On Cleveland Row," Mr. Bellamy answered for Miss Reynolds. "The Duchess of St. Edmunds is one of our members, and she has graciously consented to let us hold our meetings in her home."

"Then let us be on our way," Daniel said, his voice sounding so decisive one would have thought the entire idea his suggestion. "I am sure her grace will lend us a footman so that we might send a message to our mother. Come Penelope." He held out his arm commandingly, and she had no choice but to take it.

She shot him a mutinous look. "You think yourself very clever, don't you?" she muttered, falling into step behind the others.

Daniel's grin was piratical. "Clever enough, my dear," he responded, giving her hand a condescending pat. "Clever enough."

11

Cleveland Row was a short distance from Picadilly, but both Miss Reynolds and Mr. Bellamy expressed such horror at the thought of walking that Daniel finally gave in and flagged down a passing hackney. Because of the traffic choking the narrow streets, the carriage ride took far longer than walking would have done, and the added time gave Daniel the opportunity to reflect over what had transpired between Penelope and himself.

Why the devil did I kiss her? he brooded, listening half-attentively as Miss Reynolds prattled on about the other speakers who would be addressing the meeting. He was the man, and the responsibility for preserving Penelope's reputation as well as her virtue was his, a responsibility he had badly bungled. Had anyone walked in and discovered them in that passionate embrace, the fiction of their being brother and sister would have been destroyed beyond any hope of repair. Indeed, the scandal would have been so great, he would have been left no choice but to offer for her.

Not that it followed she would accept, of course. His lips lifted in a slight smile. Penelope was a law unto herself, and there was no telling how she might respond. She was so cursedly independent, chances were she would have hurled his offer back in his face, and boxed his ears for his efforts. He could see her now: her hazel eyes flashing fire, and that sweet, soft mouth firmed in outraged indignation . . .

His smile faded, his body responding to the memory of that soft mouth moving seductively beneath his own. At thirty-five he had enjoyed more than his share of women, but none of their touches, however experienced, affected him as much as Penelope's untutored response. She had been so sweet in her passion, so honest in her desire, that it had taken every ounce of willpower he possessed to end the kiss before it escalated into something he may not have been able to stop.

The realization was a sobering one, for he had always considered himself the master of his emotions. Even as a young buck full of wine and the devil he had never allowed his lusts to overrule his head, and it stunned him to know how close he had came to losing himself in the moment. Mayhap it was because he had been so long without a woman, he thought hopefully; then he sighed, admitting that even if he'd had a dozen women since returning to England, the results would have been the same. It was Penelope who stirred his senses so completely, and he wondered what he was going to do about it.

The home of the Duke and Duchess of St. Edmunds was huge by London standards, containing an enormous ballroom where the meeting was to be held. Daniel had been expecting a small group of no more than ten or twenty people, but there had to be three times that number crowded into the window-lined ballroom. He turned to Miss Reynolds in alarm.

"How many people are here?" he demanded, trying to count heads and quickly losing count.

"Oh, no more than fifty," she said, looking apologetic. "We usually have a better attendance, but the Countess of Lynnford is having a soiree this afternoon. I trust you do not mind?" She addressed the question to Penelope, who merely shrugged.

"Is there anything specific you wish me to address?" she asked. "Or am I just to say whatever comes to mind?"

"Oh, whatever you like would be fine, I am sure," Miss Reynolds said, fluttering her hands helplessly. "Although it might be nice if you discussed your brother's work. You did say you serve as his assistant, did you not?''

Penelope replied that she had, and Miss Reynolds led her off to the front of the room where a small dais had been erected. Daniel took his seat toward the back of the room, refusing Mr. Bellamy's offer to sit in the front row with the duke and duchess. He'd never liked Mr. Bellamy, and had no desire to spend any more time in his company than necessary. The man's effusive toadying was more than he could bear today.

The next hour passed in agonizing slowness for Daniel, and that he did not expire from boredom was a wonder to him. The first two speakers, both men, were as prosy as a couple of archbishops, and he thought they would never stop their droning. At first he thought his impatience was a result of his ignorance of the subject under discussion, an ignorance that was in no danger of being alieved by the torrent of words flowing from the speakers' mouths. Finally the second speaker reached the end of his lecture, and after a spattering of polite applause, Penelope took her place at the podium.

"Every day of our lives, each person here participates in scientific experimentation," she began, her lilting voice providing a welcome relief from the sonorous tones of her predecessors. "From the good wife mixing her bread dough, to the land owner deciding which crop to plant when, we all of us deal with science in one form or another. It is vital to our very existence and prosperity, and the discoveries of men like Sir Humphry Davy of the Royal Institution of Great Britain, and Mr. Tatum of the City Philosophical Society, have an even greater impact on our lives. The Age of Science is upon us, and we can not help but be the richer for it.''

She went on to list the advances being made, and listening to her made Daniel swell with pride. All around him the restless coughing and shuffling ceased, and a quick glance at his neighbors showed their rapt attention was fixed on Penelope. She spoke in simple, concise terms all could understand, and the things she spoke of seemed commonplace and yet somehow exotic at the same time. It was obvious she was enamored of her subject, and she freely shared that love with the audience. By the time she had finished, Daniel felt as if he'd been given a rare and wonderful treat.

There was a brief silence, and then the audience broke into wild applause. Cries of "Bravo!" and "Hurrah!" could clearly be heard, as the assembled guests let their approval be known. Penelope looked taken aback by their response, her cheeks pinking with pleasure as she glanced out at the audience. Her eyes met Daniel's and he gave her a quick wink, making her blush even harder.

The first man to speak walked up to the podium, patting the air in front of him as if to quiet the audience. "It is very kind of you to be so encouraging to our lovely speaker," he said, raising his voice so as to be heard. "But I must remind you this is an august body devoted to expanding the intellect. I must ask that you refrain your . . . er . . . enthusiasm. Now, have any of you any questions for either Mr. Morely or myself?"

Daniel's pleasure faded as the man's words sank in. Why, the pompous old rasher of wind! he thought furiously. It was obvious he was piqued at the reception Penelope had received, and was going to deny her the opportunity to speak. Well, to the devil with the old goat! he thought, surging to his feet. He would just see about that!

"I should like Miss Grantham to comment upon the future of steam power," he said in a loud voice. "Does she believe ships driven by steam have practical application in the future?"

Penelope looked startled and then pleased. "I—"

"I am sure Miss Grantham's opinions are most interesting," the man said, shooting Daniel a look that dripped scorn. "Unfortunately, only *members* of our society may answer questions from our guests. However, as it happens, the use of steam in commerce is a particular interest of mine, and I should be more than happy to respond to your query."

"As would I," Mr. Morely interjected, rising to his feet and strutting forward like an agitated pigeon. "Waste of time, if you want my opinion of it. Coal power; that's the answer for a sensible man."

The two speakers fell quickly to squabbling, quoting ob-

scure theorems and equations at each other in increasingly
abusive tones. Some of the audience sat back to enjoy the
performance, while others took the opportunity to make good
their escapes.

Seeing Penelope leaving the podium, Daniel hurried to follow her. He found her in the sitting room, receiving congratulations and praise with the graciousness worthy of a queen.
He waited patiently for the crowd to thin before moving forward to take her hand.

"Congratulations, my dear," he said, capturing her hand
and carrying it to his lips. "You have conquered us all."

Her lips twitched, her hazel eyes sparkling with laughter as
she smiled up at him. "Stuff!" she responded, with an inel-
egant snort. "You're just saying that because you're happy
you didn't have to speak!"

"That is so," he admitted, flashing her an unrepentant grin.
"But that still doesn't alter the fact you were nothing short of
brilliant. You are a credit to your father, Penelope Prudence,
and I know he would be very proud of you."

The laughter died in her eyes, and a soft sheen of tears
shimmered in its place. They gazed at each other for several
seconds, and Daniel felt an odd stirring in his heart that made
him glance away in confusion. He was trying to think of
something innocuous to say when they were rejoined by Miss
Reynolds and Mr. Bellamy.

"You were marvelous, Miss Grantham, simply marvelous!" Miss Reynolds gushed, pumping Penelope's hand with
unwonted exuberance. "Your wonderful speech shall be the
talk of the town by evening, I promise you! Oh, how bitterly
poor Lynette shall weep at having missed hearing you speak!"

She sounded so pleased, Daniel had to bite his lip to keep
from making a tart observation. A glance at Penelope showed
she was similarly affected, and he decided he'd better say
something before the laughter he saw dancing in her eyes
came bubbling out.

"Yes, I noticed Miss Chartfield wasn't present," he said,
contriving to look disappointed as he glanced about him. "Did
she have another engagement?"

"Oh, no!" Mr. Bellamy said, looking properly shocked.

"Dearest Lynette is devoted to her scientific societies, and she should never have missed one for so trifling a reason!"

"I hope she is not ill, then?" Penelope asked, her brows gathering in concern.

"Not precisely," Mr. Bellamy continued in his ponderous manner. "It is rather odd, though, for I was certain she and the viscount were no more than nodding acquaintances. But when I told her he had been shot, she burst into tears and fled up to her room. Her maid came down a few minutes later to say she was indisposed and would not be accompanying us."

Daniel's heart turned to stone. His whole chest hurt almost unbearably, and his blood went so cold it felt as if he had been plunged into an icy stream. He tried to speak, but there was no air in his lungs. He was struggling to breathe, when he felt a gentle touch on his arm.

"The viscount?" Penelope asked, her voice carefully modulated as she regarded Mr. Bellamy. "Do you mean Lord Burlington?"

"Yes." The younger man was staring at Daniel. "Oh, I say! He is your neighbor, isn't he? I am terribly sorry, I thought you knew of it. It was all anyone was talking about this morning."

"Is . . . is he alive?" Daniel asked, forcing the words past his lips by sheer force of will. He didn't want to think how he would respond if Bellamy said no. He would go mad, and then he would go to Haworth's house and kill him with his bare hands.

"Yes, thank the Lord," Miss Reynolds interjected, breaking her uncharacteristic silence with a sigh of relief. "The bullet passed through his shoulder without hitting a vital organ. It was footpads, you know. The filthy wretches are everywhere."

"No, it was Luddites, and he was shot in the leg," Mr. Bellamy corrected, sending Miss Reynolds a reproving look. "I heard the story from a member of my club, who heard it from a friend. His lordship will walk with a limp, they say."

Daniel didn't remember making his goodbyes. One minute he was in the duke's elegant salon, and the next he was on St. James, attempting to flag down a hackney. Penelope was at his side, not saying anything until a coach rattled to a halt in front of them.

"Do you want me to go with you?" she asked, her hazel eyes tender as she studied his face.

Daniel gazed down at her, the vague emotions he had been denying coalescing into a stunning certainty. He brushed his fingers across her cheek with a hand that wasn't quite steady. "More than I want to draw my next breath," he admitted, his voice raw with pain. "But it would be best if I go alone. I don't know what I will find when I get there, or what I will need to do afterward."

He saw her eyes darken, and knew she understood that if his brother *was* dead, he would take his revenge against the marquess. "Will you come home?" she asked, her own fingers caressing his face tenderly.

"If I can," he promised, praying silently he would be able to keep his word. "You may tell your mother what you wish, but now I must go." He shouted his brother's address to the driver and climbed inside, refusing to look at her again. If he had, he knew he would have lost his resolve and begged her to come with him. And she would have come, he realized, leaning back against the cracked leather cushions and closing his eyes. The thought was his only comfort as the rented carriage rattled its way toward Cavendish Square.

The footman who answered his pounding knock seemed disinclined to let him in, so Daniel brushed his way past him. The butler, drawn by the commotion, came hurrying from the back hall, his face set in lines of majestic outrage. "What the devil is going on here?" he demanded. Then his jaw dropped, his eyes bulging out in horror.

"It can not be!" he gasped, falling back a step and gazing at Daniel in a mixture of disbelief and fragile hope. "Mr. Warfield, is . . . is it you?"

"Yes, Burnleigh," Daniel replied, giving his family's elderly retainer an impatient nod. "Take me to Andrew. How is he?"

"He is resting, sir . . . my lord," Burnleigh stammered, struggling to adjust to the shifting balance of power in the household. "The doctor is with him at the moment, but—"

"Good, that will spare me the trouble of tracking one down," Daniel interrupted. He started toward the stairs, ignoring Burnleigh's sputtering protests.

"But sir, you should wait . . . !"

Although it had been over fifteen years since he had last been in the house, Daniel found his way to Andrew's rooms without faltering. The rooms had been his father's, and he assumed Andrew had moved into them following James's death. A servant and a young man in a black coat were bent over the massive bed when he walked in, and they both seemed startled by his arrival.

"Who are you?" the doctor demanded, his round chin firming in disapproval. "Whoever you are, I must insist you leave at once. I will not have you agitating my patient."

Daniel ignored him with lordly indifference, striding across the room until he reached the bed. Andrew was lying beneath the blankets and counterpane, his eyes closed. Daniel saw his chest rising and falling evenly in sleep, and it was only then he allowed himself to relax. He wasn't too late, he thought, and breathed a silent prayer of gratitude.

"What is my brother's condition?" he asked, nailing the doctor with a commanding stare. "Where was he shot?"

"In the arm," the doctor answered, a bewildered look crossing his face. "But how can you be his lordship's brother? I was given to understand he had no surviving relations."

Daniel was about to tell the physician it was none of his damned business, when Andrew stirred restlessly on the bed. He gave a low groan, his lashes fluttering and then slowly lifting as he focused his bleary gaze on Daniel's face.

"You—you are my brother?" he asked, his voice weak with incredulity.

Daniel wasn't in the least shamed by the tears stinging his eyes. "Yes, Andrew," he said, laying a shaking hand on his brother's forehead. "I am Daniel."

Andrew looked startled, and then his lips moved in a frail smile. "I knew it," he whispered, sounding smugly satisfied. "I took one look at you, and knew you had to be related to me in some fashion. I took you for father's by-blow at first.

You've his looks, you know," he added, sending Daniel an amused glance.

"I know." Daniel brushed back the damp hair falling across Andrew's forehead. "But you must rest now; we can talk later after you've recovered some of your strength."

Andrew's brow puckered in a scowl. "The devil with that," he announced, sounding every inch a Warfield. "I've thought you dead for most of my life, and I've a dozen questions I want to ask you. Bedamned if I'll be sent off to sleep like some puling infant."

"My lord, I must protest," the doctor said, his hands clutching the lapels of his jacket as he drew himself up to his full height. "You have suffered a serious injury and—"

"Get out!" Daniel and Andrew issued the command in unison, then exchanged rueful grins.

"It's only a flesh wound, doctor," Andrew said, his gaze never leaving Daniel's face. "And I can think of no better medicine than reacquainting myself with my brother. You may leave; you too, Joseph," he added, sending his valet a smile.

The older man was staring at Daniel as if he were Satan incarnate. "If you're sure, my lord," he said, his tone decidedly suspicious. "I shall be just outside in the hall should you have need of me."

The doctor followed the servant out, muttering about dire consequences beneath his breath, but neither Daniel nor Andrew paid him the slightest mind. They were too busy looking at each other, trying to catch up on fifteen years in a few precious seconds. The moment the door closed behind the departing doctor, Andrew breathed a heavy sigh.

"Don't suppose you'd care to tell me where you've been these last years, or how you came to be posing as a famous scientist?" he asked, looking determined. "I'm sure it must be fascinating."

"Later," Daniel said, pulling up a chair and sitting down. "First, I want to know how you were shot. Did Haworth have anything to do with it?"

Andrew's eyes widened. "You know about Haworth?"

Daniel hesitated, not wishing to implicate Polson, but decided he had no choice. In a few pithy sentences he told Andrew why he had come, and all that he had learned since his arrival. He also explained the reasons for his deception, and Andrew shook his head in disapproval.

"I can see where you'd think you would need to keep your identity a secret from others," he said, studying Daniel coolly. "But surely these reasons should not have applied to me. Or didn't you think I had a right to know you were still alive?"

Daniel squirmed uncomfortably. "I was going to tell you once I'd discovered the truth behind Richard's and James's deaths," he muttered, not certain if he liked being taken to task by his younger brother. "That was the only reason Polson agreed to help me. You were only a cub when father and I had our falling out, and it never occurred to me you might recognize me. I suppose I should have known better."

"As I say, there was something about you I recognized almost at once," Andrew said, shifting restlessly on his pillows. "Although I'll own I wasn't quite sure what your relationship to me might be. I fear I owe your Miss Grantham's mother an abject apology," he added, his eyes dancing with laughter. "I all but accused the poor lady of being Papa's paramour."

Daniel gave his brother an answering smile. "Yes, Penelope told me you had been asking some rather pointed questions."

"Speaking of your Miss Grantham, you are to be congratulated on your choice of conspirators," Andrew said, chuckling softly. "She is as loyal as she is lovely. She didn't give a thing away, however hard I pressed for information. In fact, she seemed so forthright I was beginning to doubt my own suspicions." He frowned as a sudden thought occurred to him. "Does she know who you really are?"

"I told her last night," Daniel answered, reluctant to discuss Penelope and her role in the charade. As he had with Polson, he'd made his posing as Ulysses sound like his idea, and he hated the realization he was deceiving his brother yet again. He pushed the troubling thoughts from his mind, and concentrated on Haworth and his reason for being here.

"You still haven't told me how you came to be shot," he said, folding his arms across his chest and fixing Andrew with a stern stare. "Have you any proof Haworth was involved?"

Andrew studied him for several seconds as if sensing his mendacity, and then sighed. ''None whatsoever,'' he admitted, looking grim. ''He'd dragged me to a particularly repellent gaming hell, before vanishing without a trace. I thought he might have gone upstairs with a doxy, and decided to take my leave before one of my fellow patrons slit my throat. I'd just stepped out into the alley when a footpad popped up out of nowhere to demand my money and my ring.''

''Was it the marquess?''

''Not unless he'd lost several stone; not to mention most of his teeth. Since the bastard was aiming a pistol at my head I did as he demanded, and I thought that was the end of it. I started walking away when I heard the man cock the pistol, and I jumped to one side. I almost made it; the bullet caught me in the shoulder rather than the back as it would have done.''

Daniel's hands clenched into tight fists at his brother's stark recounting of the night's events. He'd been in similarly tight places in his salad days, but those events had been the result of sheer stupidity rather than calculated viciousness. He drew several deep breaths before trusting himself to speak.

''Then I take it you were to be the victim of yet another unfortunate accident?'' he asked, his jaw tight with fury.

''So it would appear, but unfortunately for Haworth I was not,'' Andrew drawled, sounding as grim as Daniel. ''The footpad escaped after the shooting, and the Runners have told me it is doubtful he will ever be caught. Not that it matters, of course. I *know* Haworth was behind it.''

''How?'' Daniel asked, his respect for Andrew increasing with each passing second.

''I told him I knew about the ten thousand he owed Richard,'' Andrew replied. ''I also said that as gaming debts were a matter of honor between gentlemen, I would give him until the end of the month before pressing him for payment.''

''When was this?''

''Three days ago.'' Andrew rolled his shoulders, and then winced with pain. ''I thought that would give me enough time to set a trap, but apparently his lordship was more impatient than I realized. Now I shall have to proceed against him, regardless.''

Daniel leaned back in his chair. "This plan of yours," he said slowly. "Would it have been enough to convince a court Haworth was responsible for both James's and Richard's deaths?"

"It would have put a noose about his neck," Andrew said with cold satisfaction.

"Then I see no reason why you should abandon it," Daniel said, coming to a swift decision. "Tell me everything . . ."

"Really, Penelope, I wish you would tell me what the deuce is going on," Mrs. Grantham sighed, tapping her foot with marked impatience and glowering down at her silent daughter. "And do not tell me it is nothing, for I still have the use of my eyes and my wits to tell me otherwise."

Penelope gave a dispirited sigh, too heart-sick and weary to dissemble any longer. She had arrived home to find a hard-eyed man, who would give his name only as Polson, waiting for Daniel. When she told him Daniel had left for Lord Burlington's house the man departed, leaving Penelope to deal with her mother's querulous demands for information.

"I told you, Mama, Daniel learned Lord Burlington had been shot and went to see how he was," she said, rubbing her head with a tired hand. "He was most concerned, as you may imagine."

"Of course I can imagine, but that still does not explain what *that* man was doing here," Mrs. Grantham retorted sourly. "I know he is in the viscount's employ, for I recall seeing him in the village, but why should he come here demanding to see Daniel? I thought his lordship was unaware Daniel was his cousin?"

Penelope knew this was the perfect opportunity to apprise her mother of Daniel's real relationship to the viscount, but the effort was too much for her overwrought nerves. Later, she promised herself, rising listlessly to her feet.

"Where are you going?" Mrs. Grantham cried, her lips thinning in indignation. "I am not finished speaking with you yet!"

"I have already told you all I know," Penelope said quietly, feeling not so much as a twinge of remorse at deceiving her mama. "Now if you will pardon me, I should like to retire to my rooms. I have a terrible headache."

"But what about the Islingtons' party?" her mother demanded, also rising to her feet. "We are expected."

"You will just have to give them my apologies," Penelope told her, walking toward the door. "Good day, Mama; I shall see you tonight."

Penelope made her way up to her room, dismissing her maid with a wave of her hand. The moment she was alone she flung herself on her bed, burying her head in her arms and sobbing as if her heart would break.

She loved Daniel. The admission was as painful as it was sweet, for she was almost certain he did not return her feelings. Oh, he desired her; she might be a virgin, but she wasn't as innocent as all that. She knew he had been as aroused by their kiss as she had, and the knowledge was balm to her lacerated heart. If she were a less intelligent female she might have deluded herself into thinking that desire could be nurtured into something more viable, but she had been too well-taught by her papa to believe in fustian. As a scientist she had faced unpleasant facts before, and she faced them squarely now.

In the event Daniel elected to stay in England, he would be the viscount—and as such, far above her touch. The moment he assumed his rightful place, the world would know she had deceived them, and then there would be the devil to pay. She had been in London long enough to realize the nobility made their own rules, and that Daniel's role in this would be regarded as a lark, while she would be left to bear the full weight of the scandal on her own. Since it was all her idea, she did not object to the situation; nor would she blame Daniel for wishing to distance himself from her. It was the way of the world, and there was nothing she could do to change it.

If, on the other hand, Daniel kept to his original plan and returned to America, the result would be very much the same. He would be beyond her power to contact him, and she would never see him again. Neither alternative was particularly pleasing, and she indulged in another bout of tears as she considered the wasteland her future would be without him.

She had never thought to fall in love, and had told herself it did not matter. Now that she knew better, it was all she could do not to rail at the injustice of it all. It most unfair of God, she thought with an unhappy sniff, to let her fall in love with a man who did not, could not love her. The next moment, she was denying the very thought. Loving Daniel was quite the most wonderful thing to ever happen to her, and she refused to regret it, however it turned out.

She spent the rest of the afternoon brooding over her hopeless love, before deciding she was behaving like a ninnyhammer. She was an intellectual, she reminded herself, scrubbing her damp cheeks with an angry fists; it was time she started acting like it. Buoyed by a new sense of determination, she rose from the bed and rang for her maid, wondering if her mama had already left for the Islington's.

After bathing and changing into an afternoon gown of ruffled silk, she went downstairs to ask after her mother. She learned her mother had indeed left, and decided she would go call upon Miss Chartfield. Mr. Bellamy had said she'd burst into tears at hearing Lord Burlington had been shot, and she could well guess the reason behind her unhappiness. If Daniel had been harmed, she would have wailed like a banshee; and then she would have gone after whoever had hurt him like a fury.

She was about to have Carlysle send the footman for a carriage when Daniel walked into the room, and the sight of his grim face drove all thoughts of leaving from her mind. Aching with love for him, she hurried to his side.

"Are you all right?" she asked, not caring her heart was in her eyes as she gazed up at him. "Was his lordship badly hurt?"

Daniel shook his head, his fingers gentle as he brushed back a tendril of hair from her cheek. "A bullet caught him in the shoulder, but he will be all right in a few days. He knew who I was, Penelope. He said he took one look at me, and he knew." He went on to tell her every detail of his reunion, his deep voice filled with wonder.

"I am so happy for you," Penelope said, when he finished

speaking. She realized how much he had dreaded facing his brother honestly and openly after so many years, and she was ecstatic the viscount had welcomed him without reservation. Had his lordship rejected Daniel, she would have driven to his house and put another bullet in him herself.

Daniel continued stroking her cheek, his dark gaze following the lazy movement with an intensity that made her heart race with hope. She caught her breath, desire and uncertainty making her weak, as a longing for his kiss overwhelmed her. Her lashes fluttered shut, and her arms rose of their own volition to slip about his neck. She heard the breath catch in his throat, and felt his fingers tighten on her chin. In another moment she knew his lips would be on hers, and a soft moan slipped from her.

"Penelope." His breath feathered across her lips, as he bent his head over hers.

"Penelope! Penelope!" The door to the study was flung open, and her mother dashed in just as Daniel and Penelope sprang apart. Penelope took one look at her mother's ashen face and dazed eyes, and rushed to her side.

"Mama! What is it?" she demanded anxiously, her arms slipping about her mama's plump shoulders. "What has happened?"

"Is it Andrew . . . Lord Burlington?" Daniel demanded before she could answer, his green eyes filled with fear. "He hasn't had a relapse, has he?"

"What?" Mrs. Grantham looked up at him in confusion, then waved her hand weakly. "Oh no, this has nothing to do with your cousin," she said, her eyes closing in sick defeat. "It is Ulysses!"

"Ulysses?" Penelope gasped, wondering what terrible malady may have struck down her hapless brother. "He's not ill, is he?"

Her mother shook her head. "It is worse," she said, dabbing at her eyes with her crumpled handkerchief. "Much, much worse."

Penelope paled, her hand groping for Daniel's. "Do you mean he . . . he is . . ." She could not bring herself to say the word.

"Yes!" her mother sobbed, collapsing onto the settee and burying her face in her hands. "He is *here*!"

12

"Here?" Penelope echoed faintly, sitting back on her heels and regarding her mother in horror. "In London?"

"Yes!" Mrs. Grantham said, struggling visibly to compose herself. "I was at the Islingtons when I heard someone say some doddering buffoon had wandered in and was making a cake of himself. Naturally I assumed they were referring to one of the Royal Dukes, and when I looked up there he was!"

"One of the Royal Dukes?" Daniel asked, exchanging worried looks with Penelope.

"No! Ulysses!" Mrs. Grantham snapped, blowing her nose vigorously. "How he tracked me down there, I know not; I simply glanced up and he was standing in the doorway, dressed like that Spanish fellow. I tried hiding, but he'd already spotted me, and he started toward me prattling on about quests and sieges, and . . . Oh! I am ruined!" And she burst into another bout of tears.

"There, there, Mama, it will be all right," Penelope soothed, gently patting her mother's back as she tried to decide how to best handle this new disaster. Unfortunately it had never occurred to her that Ulysses would ever leave their house, and she had no contingency plans in place. She felt helpless and frustrated, as everything she had worked so hard for these past four years tottered on the brink of ruin. Always in the past she had been able to plot and scheme her way out of a dilemma, but the thought of Ulysses loose upon society was more than she could bear. She turned her head and looked beseechingly at Daniel.

He met her gaze, his green eyes dark and unfathomable, before he turned to her mother. "Where is Ulysses now?" he asked, his voice gentle. "Will he be staying with us?"

"No, may God be praised," Mrs. Grantham responded with unmaternal fervor. "He said Mayfair lacks ambiance, and he is putting up at some gothic hole in Clerkenwell with one of his friends. Although he did say he would be calling upon us once he was settled," she added, shuddering in horror at the prospect.

"Did he say why he had come?" Penelope asked, trying to force her frozen mind to function. In between acknowledging her love for Daniel and dealing with the consequences of his real identity, it had been an eventful day, and she wondered how many more shocks she would have to face before it was done.

"Yes." Her mother's eyes filled again. "And it is all my fault. I made the mistake of writing him that you were to be presented at court next week, and the great loony has taken it into his head that it is his duty to come and escort you!"

"What?" Penelope and Daniel exclaimed in unison.

"He said he brought his best suit of armor with him," her mother continued, her bottom lip wobbling as she bit back a sob. "He also said something about his lance, but I was too upset to make sense of it. Not that anything Ulysses *ever* says makes any sense, mind you," she added with an aggrieved growl.

They discussed the matter for several more minutes, before Daniel rose to his feet. "I think it might be best if I talk to him myself; then perhaps I can convince him to return to Bibury. You say no one else knows who he is?" he asked, glancing at Mrs. Grantham for confirmation.

She gave a weak nod, her hand clutched to her head. "Yes; he announced himself only as an errant knight. That and his outlandish clothing kept the rest of the room at bay, and I am almost positive no one heard him call me mama."

"Then we are safe enough for the moment. If you will give me the friend's address, I will go there at once," Daniel said, sounding decisive. "Will you be all right?" His question was for Penelope, and she sent him a smile of gratitude.

"I shall be fine," she promised in a soft voice. She desperately wanted to kiss him, but there was no way she could do that with her mother looking on. Thinking quickly, she rose to her feet. "While mama is telling you how to contact Ulysses, I shall run upstairs and write him a note. In the event he should prove recalcitrant, you can give it to him. I'll meet you in the hall." She dashed from the room.

Penelope handed the note to Daniel the moment he walked into the hall. "I'm sorry," she said, searching his face with a worried gaze. "You shouldn't have to deal with this; not after everything that's happened with your brother. It's not fair."

He smiled slightly, the corners of his eyes wrinkling in wry amusement. "The first thing I learned is that life is seldom fair," he said, slipping his arms about her waist and drawing her close. "You and your mama have become like a family to me, so I suppose that would make Ulysses my brother as well.

"Besides," he added, his grin deepening, "I must own I am longing to meet him so I might see if he is as odd as you claim. And what did your mother mean he was dressed like a Spaniard? I thought he favored knights of old."

"Don Quixote," Penelope explained, doing her best not to cry. Hearing Daniel regarded her as a sort of honorary sister was painful in the extreme, and she clung to her composure with grim determination. "He has read the novel so many times, he can quote long passages from it at the drop of a hat. He mistook a milkmaid for Dulcena last year, and we had a devil of a time convincing him she didn't require rescuing."

"So long as he doesn't take me for Sancho Panza, we should rub along well enough," Daniel quipped, then looked somber. "Are you quite sure you're all right?" he asked, studying her anxiously. "Your eyes look as if you have been crying."

Penelope's cheeks reddened. "Tears of anger, more like," she said, giving a shaky laugh. "Now be off with you, before my foolish brother mistakes the Tower of London for a wind-mill and decides to attack it.''

She saw the devil dancing in his eyes, then he bent his head and pressed a quick, hard kiss on her mouth. ''A token of my lady's affection,'' he said, his thumb moving over her lips in a teasing caress. ''We knights never go into battle without one.''

Only her pride kept Penelope's knees from folding beneath her. She managed a shaky smile as she tipped back her head to study him. ''So you are a knight now as well, hmm?'' she drawled, congratulating herself on her aplomb.

He cocked an eyebrow rakishly. ''I'm supposed to be Ulysses, aren't I?'' he asked, his tone deliberately provocative.

''Beast.'' She gave his shoulder a playful punch and then sent him a worried look. ''Will—will you be coming directly home?''

The laughter faded from his face. ''No, I'm spending the evening with Andrew,'' he said, his arms dropping as he took a step back. ''We have a great deal to discuss.''

''Yes, I can imagine,'' she agreed, determined to be as non-chalant as he was. ''Shall I see you tomorrow, then?''

''Of course. We're rehearsing the demonstration one final time, remember?''

Penelope started as she realized that between Daniel's shocking revelation and Ulysses's appearance, the rehersal had slipped her mind. She was about to thank him for the reminder when the worry shadowing his eyes stopped her.

''If you would prefer spending the day with his lordship, I quite understand,'' she said, unable to keep from touching him as she lay her hand on his arm. ''Besides, the actual demonstration won't be for many more days yet, and—''

''Actually,'' Daniel interrupted, placing his hand over hers, ''I've been thinking, and with Ulysses running about, I feel it would be best to hold the presentation as soon as it can be arranged. With all that has gone on, we can ill-afford your brother creating a scandal by announcing his true identity.''

That made sense, and yet Penelope couldn't help but feel dismayed. The presentation was their main reason for being in London; with that behind them they would have no reason to stay, and Daniel would naturally expect them to return to Bibury. The thought brought a painful lump to her throat.

"Penelope?" Daniel studied her with obvious concern. "Is something wrong?"

She quickly averted her head, fearing he would see the love she bore him reflected in her eyes. "Of course something's wrong, you wretch," she retorted, fixing a scowl on her face as she glanced back at him. "If you mean to hold the presentation at once, I shall have to spend the rest of the night going over my notes. Now, take yourself off so that I might get started."

Her tart observation won a soft chuckle from him. "As you wish, my lady," he drawled, his eyes bright with laughter. "By the by, what was in your note to Ulysses, if you do not mind my asking?"

"Not at all," Penelope answered, relieved he accepted her reply. "I merely wrote we were quite looking forward to seeing him again, and that he mustn't pay the slightest attention to the rumor our maid has contracted the fever. I assured him I was *almost* certain she wasn't contagious."

Daniel look puzzled, and then shot her a grin. "And given your brother's horror of disease, nothing could be more certain to keep him as far from you as possible. Brilliant, my little termagant; you are as devious as you are lovely." He caught her hand and raised it to his lips for a brushing kiss. "Goodbye, Penelope; I shall see you tomorrow."

Penelope remained in the hall long after he had gone, wondering why such a blatant insult should have sounded so much like an endearment. That's what falling in love did to one, she concluded with an unhappy sigh, her shoulders drooping as she dragged herself back into the parlor where her mama was waiting. It left one mooning after the most ridiculous things . . .

Daniel went to the home in Clerkenwell where Ulysses was staying, but to his disappointment he had already gone out for the evening. He left the note with the butler, and with his obligations to the Granthams concluded, he returned to Cavendish Square where he found Andrew sitting up in bed and enjoying a meal of rare steak and ale. "I am gratified to see you are feeling better," he said, lowering himself on a chair and eyeing his brother with approval. "Shall I send for an opera dancer to complete the celebration?"

"Later, perhaps," Andrew replied, his grin much like Daniel's own. "I'd as lief my arm didn't throb every time I put it about a pretty girl's waist, if you do not mind."

"As you wish," Daniel agreed, folding his arms across his chest as he settled back to discuss the reason for his visit. "I have been thinking about your plan to trap Haworth," he began, "and I've decided it will not serve."

Andrew paused, his fork poised a few inches from his mouth. "Why the devil not?" he demanded, his brows meeting as he lowered his fork. "He already knows I am holding his vowels. Why shouldn't I use them to force him into admitting he killed James and Richard? It is the only way we can hope to catch him."

"Allow me to rephrase," Daniel corrected, inclining his head coolly. "It isn't the plan I object to, as much as the participants. Haworth's had one go at killing you; I'm not about to provide him with another. I shall go in your stead."

Andrew brought his fist down on his tray, making the cutlery leap and his glass of ale go flying. "Blast it, Daniel, you have no right! The bastard murdered my brothers—"

"They were my brothers as well," Daniel interrupted, letting the violence of his fury show for the first time. "You had years with them I never had because of Father's damnable lies, and then Haworth stole the rest from me. They are dead because of him, and if it is the last thing I do, I shall make him pay for what he has done. So do not talk to me of rights, Andrew, because you have no idea what the hell you are talking about!"

Andrew leaned back against his pillows, his eyes filling with grudging respect. "I remember Father once said you had a temper blacker than the devil's own, and it seems he didn't exaggerate. Remind me not to provoke you again."

"If I have a temper, it is no less black than his," Daniel answered, his shoulders relaxing as his anger faded. "Regarding your plan, have you sent for a Runner as we discussed?

Having an impartial witness hearing Haworth's confession is a good idea, but having one with ties to the courts is even better.''

"I sent Bow Street a note, but I've yet to hear back," Andrew said, deferring to Daniel as if he had been doing so all his life. "On the other hand, I *have* heard from Haworth."

"What?" Daniel demanded, sitting forward in outrage.

In answer, Andrew handed him a note that had arrived by special messenger. Daniel unfolded it, his eyes narrowing as he read the missive. "The black-hearted whoreson," he muttered, his fingers crumpling the note. "He does not lack for cheek, does he? How dare he hint that he had warned you against the dangers of gaming hells, when he's the one who took you there?"

"He could scarce admit he had lured me there and then arranged to have me killed, could he?" Andrew drawled, cocking his eyebrow in amusement. "As far as he knows, he still has me neatly under his thumb—a delusion I am willing to let stand for the moment."

Daniel merely grunted, drumming his fingers against his knee as he considered the matter. If Haworth had been desperate enough to make such a blatant attempt on Andrew's life, then it followed that the longer he was loose, the more danger Andrew would be in. Having lost Richard and James, Daniel wasn't about to risk having anything befall his remaining brother as well. For Andrew's sake, Haworth had to be eliminated now.

"I will go to Bow Street tomorrow morning," he said at last, his stomach tightening as cold resolve settled inside him. "If they agree to lend us a man, I want you to invite Haworth to dinner tomorrow night. Tell him you have a surprise for him."

"What sort of surprise?"

"Me." Daniel's eyes glittered with malicious pleasure. "How do you think his lordship will react when he learns the prodigal son has returned to claim his title, and all that goes with it—including the ten thousand pounds he owed Richard?"

Andrew frowned as he considered the marquess's possible

reaction. "He'll probably swoon," he guessed, his lips twisting in a calculating smile. "And then he'll do his best to win you over to his side."

"Which I will make plain can only be accomplished one way," Daniel finished for him. "And that is for him to kill you."

"Me?" Andrew looked both alarmed and intrigued.

"Of course. For added measure I'll tell him I know he killed Richard and James, and that I prefer he finish the job. He'll not only admit to being responsible for their deaths, but he'll also agree to arrange yours, and the moment he does that we'll have him. We'll have him right here," Daniel raised his clenched hand for emphasis, "and then I will crush him."

They spent the next two hours arranging the necessary details and making counterplans in case Bow Street proved uncooperative. Daniel was relieved to see that beneath Andrew's indolent facade he was both shrewd and dedicated, qualities Daniel felt certain would grow even more pronounced as he matured. They were discussing recruiting a member of the House of Lords Andrew felt could be trusted, when Andrew suddenly frowned.

"Good gad, I have just thought of something," he said, regarding Daniel with shock. "You really *are* the viscount!"

"No, I'm not."

"Of course you are," Andrew insisted. "You're the oldest surviving son; that makes you the viscount."

"But I didn't survive," Daniel said, the agonizing indecision he had been dealing with since returning to England settling at last into comforting certainty. "There is a headstone in Bibury to that effect, remember? And despite what the resurrectionists might believe, the dead do not rise to walk again."

"But—"

"Andrew." Daniel leaned forward and took his brother's hand. "I have already discussed this with Polson, and I will tell you what I told him. I am an American now. My life is there, and the moment Haworth has been dealt with, I am returning home."

"What about me?" Despite the fact he was a man grown,

Andrew's question sounded much like the demand of a worried child.

"I can still return for visits, or you can come to Charleston," Daniel said, touched by his brother's wish to remain in contact. "Do not think you will be rid of me forever."

They talked for another hour or so, until Daniel saw Andrew was tiring. "If you will excuse me, I believe I shall be returning to my temporary family," he said, squeezing Andrew's arm as he rose to his feet. "I have a great deal to do if I am to be ready for the demonstration. That reminds me, where is Polson?"

"He is the one I sent to plague Bow Street," Andrew said. "I figured with his connections he was the best man for the job."

"Ah yes, Polson's connections." Daniel frowned thoughtfully. "I have always wondered about those. Any idea how a common steward is able to command such power?"

"Probably because he is an uncommon steward," Andrew said with a chuckle. "Richard once told me Polson is a by-blow of the old king's brother, and that his Highness personally arranged his position with Father."

Daniel thought of Polson's pale blue eyes and laughed. "That would explain it, then," he said, shaking his head ruefully. "How it must have made Father crow to have a steward with royal blood flowing through his viens."

He and Andrew spoke for several more minutes and then Daniel took his leave, promising to return the next afternoon. It was only as he was in the carriage making his way back to South Audley Street, that he realized this was the first time he had spoken of his father without feeling anger or bitterness. The realization had him contemplating a great deal as the coach rattled down the cobblestone streets toward home.

"Blast it to flinters!" Penelope exclaimed, tossing down her quill in disgust. She'd spend the past three hours poring over her notes, and they made less sense now than when she'd started. Obviously any further attempts at study would be a waste of time, and the realization added to her acrid mood.

This was all Daniel's fault, she decided, rising to her feet to pace. If thoughts of him hadn't kept intruding while she was working, she would have finished her new equations hours ago. It seemed to her that as she was making this heroic effort on the wretch's behalf, the least he could do was to keep out of her mind. How was she to accomplish anything when all she could think of was him?

No, that wasn't fair, she admitted with an unhappy sigh. The fault, to paraphrase Shakespeare, lay not with Daniel, but with her and her foolish heart. If she didn't want to fall into a decline like the foolish heroine out of a Minervian novel, she would have to face her love for Daniel and then put it behind her. How she was to do that, she did not know; she only knew she had to try or go quietly mad.

With that decision made she returned to her desk, this time succeeding in blocking everything from her mind but the equations she had scribbled on a scrap of paper. Since the day she and Daniel had visited the Royal Society's laboratory, she had been working on a new formula that would explain how the wire became magnetized. She felt once she could explain that, she would be able to better prove the connect between the two forces.

She was sketching out an idea for a new apparatus when the door to her study was pushed open, and Daniel walked into the room. "What are you doing still awake?" he asked, his brows gathering in a frown as he advanced toward her. "It's gone past one in the morning."

"I am working on a new theory," she replied, her heart racing at the sight of him. "As I said earlier, I've a great deal to do if you mean to move up the demonstration to this week."

"Yes, but that doesn't mean you need to burn yourself to the nub," he said, his voice gently scolding. "You will make yourself ill if you drive yourself too hard."

His concern filled Penelope with hope, even as her more rational self argued he was merely being polite. "I'm almost finished," she answered, turning away from him to pick up her sketch. "I'm considering using a copper disc in the first part of the experiment to see what effect it has upon the needle. What do you think?"

He reached out and plucked the paper from her hand. "I

think," he began, leaning so close his breath feathered across her cheek, "that it is time you were abed. I will not have you making yourself ill over this."

His nearness had the breath clogging in her throat, and it was several seconds before she could trust herself to speak. "It sounds as if you mean to play the dictatorial brother again," she said, striving for an casualness she was far from feeling.

He placed the sketch on the desk and drew back, his gaze holding hers. "I'm not playing," he told her, his voice taking on a soft, seductive tone that had her senses rioting. "And I'm not your brother."

Penelope moistened her lips, her arms lifting of their own volition to rest on his broad shoulders. "I—I know that," she stammered, threading her fingers through his dark hair. The sketch forgotten, the only magnetism interesting her now was that which flowed between her and Daniel.

"Do you?" Daniel asked, and then his lips were on hers, burning her with the blazing depths of his passion.

Penelope responded eagerly, tilting back her head and granting him the access his hungry mouth demanded. She knew she was placing herself beyond the pale with her wanton behavior, but she refused to care. She loved Daniel with all her heart, and knowing this was all she might ever have of him made her determined to take whatever he was willing to offer.

"Penelope," he groaned, his voice raw as he crushed her to him. She could feel his body shaking, and she revelled in the knowledge he desired her as much as she desired him. Her hands slid deeper into his hair, instincts as old as time guiding her. When he deepened the kiss, she welcomed his intimate touch with a soft sigh of pleasure.

They continued kissing and touching, and Penelope felt a sharp stab of disappointment when Daniel finally drew back. Her unhappiness was only slightly lessened by the fact that he looked as frustrated and reluctant to end their caresses as she felt.

"We must talk," he said, his rough voice contrasting sharply with the gentleness in his hands as he brushed the tumbled hair back from her cheeks. "When all of this nonsense is behind us, we must talk.'' And before Penelope could gather her breath to ask him what he wished to discuss, he was gone.

Daniel spent a restless night grappling with the realization that he had come dangerously close to compromising the lady he loved. Had the kiss proceeded any further, Penelope would have been well within her rights to demand marriage of him: a prospect that filled him more with wonder than horror. He adored Penelope, and nothing would give him greater pleasure than to make her his bride. Unfortunately, until the situation with Haworth was resolved he had neither a name nor a future to offer her, and he refused to go to her without them.

It was nearing dawn before he managed to drift into sleep, and it seemed he'd no sooner closed his eyes than he was being shaken awake.

"Mr. Grantham! Mr. Grantham! You must get up, sir!''

Daniel peeled open a bleary eye, blinking until his valet's face swam into focus. "What the devil are you doing, Frederick?'' he demanded grouchily, his eye already closing. "Take yourself off and let me sleep.''

"But Mr. Grantham, you have an urgent message from Lord Burlington!'' Frederick gave him another shake. "You are wanted there at once!''

The mention of his brother's name brought Daniel's eyes snapping open, and he bolted up in bed. "Is his lordship all right?'' Andrew had seemed fine when he'd left last evening, but that didn't mean he couldn't have suffered a relapse. Or worse still, that Haworth hadn't managed to get to him a second time and finish what the footpad had started.

"The messenger did not say, Mr. Grantham. He said only that you should come as soon as it was possible,'' Frederick said, holding out a dressing gown for Daniel.

The information did little to lessen Daniel's anxiety, and he leapt out of bed to begin dressing. He paused to dash off a quick note to Penelope, explaining the situation and promising to return the moment he was able. That done, he ran out into the street and caught a hackney to Cavendish Square.

He arrived to find Andrew much improved, sitting up in a

chair and plotting strategy with Polson. When Andrew glanced up and saw him standing in the doorway, he greeted him with a brotherly grin of welcome.

"You're late," he charged, green eyes dancing with suppressed excitement. "Polson and I have already worked out the details on how we shall capture Haworth. Haven't we, Polson?"

"Most of 'em, my lord," the cagey Irishman agreed, tipping his head in Daniel's direction. "A good day to you, Mr. Warfield," he said, his accent more lilting than usual. "A pleasure it is, to be seeing you and your brother together again."

"And a pleasure it is for us as well," Daniel drawled, taking his place in the group of conspirators. "But what do you mean you have worked out the details of Haworth's capture? I thought it was decided last night that I should be the one to nab him."

"To help nab him, sir," Polson corrected, surprisingly pedantic. "Only a Runner or a constable may lay hands on a man and hold him for the court's pleasure, and even then he runs the risk of having a charge of false arrest placed on him. You're the bait in the trap; the Runners I'll have in place will be the teeth. 'Tis safer that way."

Daniel frowned at the chiding note in the steward's voice. "I'm not afraid of Haworth."

"Dare say you're not, Mr. Warfield. But if you was to be the one to charge the marquess, you'd be required to give your true name—something I understand you'd as lief not be doing."

"I still say *I* should be the bait," Andrew said before Daniel could speak. "The devil had me shot; it seems to me I am entitled to the pleasure of seeing him clapped in irons."

"Nay, lad," Polson disagreed, laying his hand on Andrew's good shoulder. "You're the viscount. You owe it to the land and the people not to be taking any foolish risks. And 'twill be better the way Mr. Warfield has planned it. A blackguard would never suspect another blackguard the way he would an honest man, and he'll be more easily caught if he thinks your brother is as dishonest a villain as himself."

Andrew made a face. "Your argument, Polson, is convoluted enough to make sense. Very well, Daniel, Haworth is all yours; just mind you don't kill him before the law has their chance with him. I should hate to have you brought back from the dead only to swing."

They spent the rest of the morning going over the very tidy trap they were arranging for the marquess, perfecting each point until any possibility of a mistake had been eliminated. To give them time to have everything in place, it was decided the confrontation would take place the next evening, a change in plans that had Daniel chomping on the bit.

"I would prefer we get this over as soon as possible," he confided in Polson as they were sharing a private moment while Andrew dressed. "What's to stop Haworth from attacking Andrew outright? You did say he was desperate."

"Aye, but not a fool," Polson said grimly. "He'll doubtless be content to bide his time and spin a better web like the spider that he is. And I'll have Runners watching the house as well, if that shall reassure you."

"It does," Daniel said, giving him a grateful smile. "Thank you, Polson, you make an admirable conspirator."

"And you, Mr. Warfield, make an admirable viscount," Polson said, then held up his hands before Daniel could speak. "I know you said the title was Andrew's, and after seeing him deal with the marquess, I am of the opinion the lad will do well. But that doesn't change the fact the title would rest easier on your head than his."

Daniel remained silent, allowing himself to contemplate the idea of Burlington being his. He knew Andrew would stand aside without a moment's hesitation, but to his relief the thought wasn't even the slightest bit tempting. He loved Andrew, and he would forever mourn his brothers and his parents, but the past was well and truly behind him. Until this moment, he had no idea how heavy a burden it had been.

"Perhaps you are right," he agreed, his gaze meeting Polson's, "but my answer is the same as it has always been. Andrew is welcome to Burlington; I wish him naught but success with it."

Polson studied him a long moment before nodding his head. "Aye, I can see that you do, lad, and may I say I am glad to see it? Hating the past only poisons the future; that I learned only after years of bitterness. Now," he added brusquely, looking as if he feared becoming maudlin, "is there nothing else I can be doing for you? Will you be needing help arranging passage back to Charleston?"

Daniel shook his head, neglecting to mention he owned a fleet of packet ships. "No, that is all arranged," he said, then paused. "Actually, there is something you can do for me."

"What is it, sir?"

Daniel explained about the demonstration and the need to hold it as soon as possible. Polson chuckled over his dilemma, and then rose to his feet, clapping Daniel on the back.

"I'll see to it at once," he promised, blue eyes twinkling. "There is just one favor I would be asking of you."

"What is that?" Daniel asked, equally amused by Polson's puckish behavior.

"That you introduce me to the real Ulysses Grantham," Polson said, giving Daniel a sly wink. "The one I met is a dull as ditchwater fellow, and I'd much rather make the acquaintance of the genuine article. 'Tis a bit of the Irish he must have, to be so fanciful. The saints know you English never had so fine a sense of the ridiculous."

13

Penelope was hard at work in her study when Daniel walked in. She glanced up, her eyes bright with the joy of seeing him.

"I have it, Daniel!" she exclaimed, her cheeks flushing with delight. "The magnet does not effect the current; the current effects the magnet! It electrifies it!"

Daniel frowned, her words apparently making little sense to him. She was about to explain when he snapped his fingers with understanding. "Do you mean you'll be able to prove your theory?" he asked, advancing into the room to study the notations she'd scrawled on a scrap of paper.

"No, but it means you will be able to prove it in my stead," she said, triumph making her giddy. The solution to why the needle hadn't moved in the direction she expected had come to her the moment she'd opened her eyes, and she'd spent a frantic morning trying to prove it. The answer would give her original theory a dramatic twist, but as far as she was concerned, that was what made science so exciting. One could take precautions and calculate every step to the finest degree, and still end up being caught unawares. Rather like life, she decided, her gaze sliding in Daniel's direction.

"This is interesting," he said, his attention fixed on her notes. "But isn't it rather late to be switching theories? I've only just become comfortable with your original thesis, and now you are thrusting a new one on me. I'll sound like a babbling fool standing up there trying to make sense of this.''

''That will only add to the drama,'' she assured him, giving his arm a comforting pat. ''You will explain that this new premise has only just occurred to you, and beg their indulgence for any mistake you might make.''

He looked thoughtful for a moment, and then his eyes gleamed with a mixture of amusement and respect. ''What a devious mind you have, my love,'' he said, flicking his finger down her nose. ''I thank heaven you are so law-abiding; one shudders to think what might happen should you turn your intellect to criminal pursuits.''

His words as well as his touch brought a flush of pleasure to Penelope's cheeks. She supposed a true lady would be horrified at being accused of harboring felonious proclivities, but she was delighted. His teasing observation meant far more to her than the easy endearment he had uttered, for she knew it to be genuine. When he was gone, it would be one of the precious memories she would hoard in the empty years ahead.

The thought of those empty years brought a swift stab of pain to her heart, and she turned quickly away. ''I got your note this morning,'' she said briskly, her hands trembling as she stacked the paper on her desk. ''How is Andrew? I trust he is recovering from his wounds?''

''He's up and about and itching for revenge,'' Daniel replied, sounding well-pleased with his brother's progress. ''We have laid a trap for Haworth, and with luck the authorities shall have him in custody within the next forty-eight hours.''

She considered his reply for an agonizing moment. ''And if luck is not with you?'' she asked, fearing his reply. ''What then?

There was a taut silence behind her and then Daniel's hands were on her shoulders, turning her to face him. ''There's a risk,'' he admitted quietly, his restless green gaze moving over her face. ''I won't lie to you about that. But we'll have Bow Street Runners in place before Haworth arrives, so the danger will be minimal. Don't worry.'' His lips quirked in a half-smile. ''I'll still be here to pose as Ulysses for you.''

Anger and hurt flashed through Penelope. ''Do you think I

care about that now?'' she demanded, blinking back furious tears. ''You could be killed, blast you!''

His hands slid up from her shoulders to cup her face, his expression unfathomable as he gazed down at her. ''And that would matter?'' he asked, moving his thumb across her trembling mouth in a gentle caress.

Penelope knew she should demur, but she knew also this could well be the last time he would hold her. The strict morality she'd been raised with faded into insignificance compared to the love blazing inside her, and she looped her arms about his neck. ''It matters,'' she said softly, her lashes drifting closed when she felt his breath feathering across her lips. ''It matters more than I can ever tell you.''

Daniel gave a soft groan and then his lips were on hers, sweeping her away on a sweet, warm tide of desire.

''Now remember, lad, it's no heroics we'll be wanting from you this night. Just stay to the plan we've worked out, and we'll soon have that *deamhan* were we want him,'' Polson instructed, his expression grim as he studied Daniel's face. They were sitting in Andrew's study, sharing a companionable glass of brandy and going over their strategy as they awaited Haworth's arrival.

''I'll be as cautious as a spinster with her virtue,'' Daniel replied, suppressing the cold fury welling in him. He knew if Polson even suspected how eager he was for the coming confrontation, he would cancel everything without a moment's hesitation. They had come too far and worked too hard to back away now, so he kept his face expressionless with icy determination.

''You certainly look the part of the disreputable son returned home to claim his inheritance by fair means or foul,'' Andrew observed laconically, leaning back in his chair and observing Daniel with approval. ''It's a good thing I know you have no real designs on Burlington, otherwise I'd be looking over my shoulder with genuine trepidation.''

''I am glad my appearance pleases your lordship,'' Daniel drawled, his gaze flicking to the pier glass above the mantel. He was dressed in a finely tailored coat of black velvet, a large sapphire winking in the folds of his elegantly tied cravat. The sapphire was his own, something he had purchased on a whim, but the gold signet ring glittering on his finger was Andrew's. It bore the crest of his family, and wearing it added credence to his claim he had arrived to take the title that was rightly his.

A servant, who was a Runner in disguise, arrived to announce the marquess, and Andrew turned to Daniel. "Are you ready?" he asked, unable to keep the anticipation out of his voice.

Daniel's own excitement escalated, and he coldly tamped it down. "As ready as I shall ever be," he replied, mentally bracing himself. This was the moment he had been yearning for since standing before his brothers' graves, yet oddly it wasn't Richard or James in his thoughts. It was Penelope, and the memory of the burning kiss they had shared this morning that was uppermost in his thoughts.

The kiss had been glorious, arousing and delighting him with its undisguised passion. Although he hadn't allowed it to evolve into anything more scandalous, the kiss had given him the hope that Penelope's emotions for him were as strong as were his for her. Only the looming confrontation with Haworth prevented him from making his declaration, and the moment they had the marquess in irons, he was determined to lay his heart at Penelope's feet.

Haworth entered the room a few minutes later, the look of fatuous concern on his face fading into confusion when he saw Daniel sprawled in the chair. "Why, Mr. Grantham, what a surprise to find you here," he said, his dark eyes darting toward Andrew. "I pray you will not think me rude, but I had hoped for a private conversation with Lord Burlington."

Daniel allowed a silence of several seconds to pass before responding. "Had you?" he drawled mockingly. "In that case, I should hate to see you disappointed." He turned his head and gave Andrew a cold look. "You may leave."

As they had rehearsed, Andrew surged to his feet, his youthful face set with fury. "As you wish, *my lord*," he said, hurling the title at Daniel contemptuously. "But don't think this is the end, not by a long chalk." With that he turned and stalked out of the study, ignoring the gaping marquess.

Daniel settled back in his chair and idly crossed his feet. "You will have to pardon my youngest brother," he said, measuring with satisfaction the horrified look that flashed across Haworth's face. "I fear he was not at all pleased to find I had returned from the land of the dead."

Haworth plopped down on the nearest chair, sweat beading his brow as he stared at Daniel. "I do not understand," he said, his voice quavering in shock. "I thought you were Ulysses Grantham."

"Appearances can be deceiving, Lord Haworth, as I am sure you well know," Daniel said, deviating slightly from the plan by not telling the marquess even the slightest detail of his masquerade.

"I am sure I have no idea as to your meaning, sir," Haworth responded haughtily, but Daniel could see the panic in his eyes. "You and that cub Andrew are having a laugh at my expense, that is what. And while I appreciate a lark as well as the next man, I must insist—"

"I'd hardly call ten thousand pounds a lark." Daniel inserted the sum with the skill of a fencer sliding his blade into an opponent. "Especially to a man whose pockets are as to let as yours. That *is* the amount you owed Richard, is it not?" he added, his eyebrows arching as Haworth gasped in dismay.

"I . . . I . . . how did you know about that?" Haworth stammered, panic darkening his eyes.

Daniel smiled. "The depth of my knowledge, my lord, would truly amaze you. For example, I know you killed both Richard and James, and that a few nights ago you tried your hand at killing Andrew as well."

A retching noise slipped from the marquess, and Daniel wondered cynically if Haworth was about to be ill all over Andrew's Aubusson carpet. "That is a lie, a foul lie," Haworth sputtered, trying to sound outraged, but sounding more like a terrified schoolboy facing a brutal headmaster. "I shall bring charges against you for daring to utter such slander."

"Not that I am complaining, mind," Daniel continued, ignoring Haworth's threat with bored indifference. "I should never have inherited had you not been so obliging as to clear the path for me. Of course, I might have wished you had been a tad bit more successful in the last attempt. Now getting rid of Andrew shall be twice as dicey.''

There was a charged silence, and Daniel was certain he could hear the marquess's thoughts shifting from terror to fragile hope. "What do you mean?" he asked, squirming uneasily. "I had naught to do with—"

"Please," Daniel interrupted, holding up his hand with a sigh, "do not test either my patience or my intellect. I have enough proof to see you dangling from a gibbet, if that is my pleasure, and I would caution you against annoying me. I can not bear to be annoyed.''

It was odd and a little sickening to see the slow respect stealing into Haworth's mud-colored eyes. "Then why haven't you handed me over to the constables?" he asked in a sly voice. "Perhaps your proof isn't as sound as you think.''

Daniel wondered if the marquess was aware he had more or less tacitly confessed to two murders. But it wasn't enough, not nearly enough, and Daniel moved silently in for the kill. "Then you won't mind waiting while I send one of the servants for the watch, will you?" he asked silkily, then smiled as Haworth paled. "I thought as much.''

There was a taut silence, and then Haworth slumped in his chair. "Don't know how you tumbled to it," he complained, his bottom lip protruding in a petulant pout. "Except for some fool of a steward, no one else suspected a thing.''

Daniel's hands clenched into fists, but he kept the same bored expression stamped on his face. "Did they not?" he asked, infusing a mocking note in his voice. "I seem to recall hearing any number of the most interesting rumors. Did you really think a third Viscount Burlington could die in your vicinity and not have someone become a trifle curious?''

Haworth shrugged his shoulders defensively. "Talk means nothing without proof," he grumbled, "and I thought I'd made dashed sure there was none to be had.''

Daniel's heart began pounding in excitement. With every word Haworth was weaving the noose that would be slipped about his neck, but he still hadn't come right out and confessed. He wanted there to be no chance at all his lordship could escape justice, and to do that he would need him caught in a net so tightly he would have no hope in hell of wriggling free. He took a deep breath to steady himself.

"Yes, I must say you were indeed clever in making Richard's and James's deaths look like acts of nature, but your attack on Andrew bordered on the farcical. Luring him to a notorious gaming hell and then abandoning him to his fate; really, what could you have been thinking? If you want your vowels back from me, you shall have to do much better than that."

He saw the cunning light spring to life in the marquess's eyes. Haworth licked his lips, obviously tasting the sweet wine of deliverance from his dilemma. "What do you mean, my lord?"

Daniel held himself rigidly. The door to Haworth's right was inching open, and he knew the others were getting into position. He paused, as much for effect as to savor his victory, and gave Haworth a slow smile. "Prior to your arrival, Andrew made it plain he means to challenge my right to the title," he said coolly. "I should find such a challenge inconvenient, and I should be grateful to the tune of, shall we say, ten thousand pounds should he meet with another, more successful accident. Do you understand what I am saying?"

"You want me to kill him for you?" Haworth's greed was only surpassed by his stupidity. "I should be happy to, my lord. Damned puppy cost me fifty bob. That's how much the filthy cutpurse I hired charged me, and he didn't even do a proper job of it."

Satisfaction and fury exploded in Daniel's veins at his artless confession. "Then I hope you prove more reliable than your hirelings," he said coolly, tensing as he asked the question that would convict Haworth beyond any shadow of doubt.

"There is just one thing I do not understand," he drawled, managing to look indifferent, "and that is why you felt it neccesary to kill them. Granted ten thousand pounds is a great deal of money, but surely had you explained you were unable to honor your vowels, my brothers would have understood."

"And risk having it bandied about the clubs I had welshed

on my gaming debts?'' Haworth looked horrified. ''Don't be daft, sir, I should have been ruined as a gentleman. I had to kill them; it would not have been fair to allow them to destroy me.''

We have him! Daniel thought exultantly, although his expression didn't alter by so much as a flicker. ''So long as you had cause,'' he said, rising languidly to his feet and offering the marquess his hand. When Haworth took it, that would be the Runners signal to close in.

''Come, my lord,'' he said, smiling as Haworth also rose. ''Let us shake hands on our arrangement, like gentlemen.''

Haworth accepted his hand, good will and delight fairly oozing from him. ''As you wish, sir,'' he said, his voice so cheerful one would think he was sealing an agreement for trade, rather than agreeing to a foul act of murder. ''I shall look forward to doing business with you.''

Daniel smiled again, watching the pleasure on Haworth's face dissolve into horror as the Runners surged forward from their hidden positions. He turned on Daniel, his eyes wide with desperation. ''You bloody bastard!'' he wailed, as the men closed in on him. ''You gulled me!''

''I know,'' Daniel said genially and then doubled up his fist, striking the other man with as much power as he could muster. He was raising his hand for a second blow when Andrew grabbed his arm, staying him.

''No more, Daniel,'' he said, his voice low-pitched so as not to be overheard by the others who were busy shackling the loudly protesting marquess. ''We have him; let that be enough for now.''

Daniel watched, narrowed-eyed as Haworth was led away. ''When I see him hanging, then it will be enough,'' he said, then glanced back at Andrew. ''You heard him?''

Andrew nodded grimly. ''I did, and more importantly, so did the Runners. Haworth may deny and protest all he wishes, and he won't be able to wiggle free. It's over.''

Daniel thought of Richard and James, both dead because of one man's cowardice and greed, and felt tears stinging his eyes. With Haworth in custody he could say his mental good-byes to them, knowing he had done all he could for them.

Now he could return home and get on with his life.

As if sensing his thoughts Andrew placed a brotherly arm about his shoulders. "They will rest easier now, Daniel," he said quietly. "And so will I. One of the reasons their deaths were so hard to take was because I thought it meant I was all alone in the world." His green eyes met Daniel's. "Now I know I am not."

Daniel's eyes burned with tears. "No," he agreed rawly. "You're not." And he caught his brother in a fierce embrace.

The news of Haworth's arrest spread quickly through the *ton*. Although everyone seemed genuinely scandalized a peer would soon be standing trial for murder, no one, they assured Penelope, was *really* surprised. They had all known he was a blackguard, and that he would hang seemed a forgone conclusion.

To her chagrin it had proved impossible to keep Daniel's involvement in the affair quiet, as he would be required to give testimony at Haworth's trail. Fortunately Mr. Polson explained away his participation by saying Bow Street had made use of his resemblance to the viscount to fool the marquess into thinking he was the long-dead Daniel Warfield. This naturally made him or rather Ulysses something of a hero, and the day of the demonstration, the lecture hall was filled to overflowing with the cream of London society.

Penelope stood at the podium beside Daniel, shaking with terror at the sheer size of the crowd facing them. "We shall never be able to carry this off," she whispered, hating the fear that was making her stomach pitch and roll like a tiny sloop caught in the maws of a powerful storm. "They shall see through us at once, and laugh us out of London."

He reached down and captured her icy fingers in his. "Don't worry," he said, shooting her a reassuring smile. "We've been over this a dozen times in the last three days, and I have every faith in you and your abilities. It will be fine, I promise."

His confidence comforted her, as Penelope knew he intended, but it did little to remove the unhappiness welling inside her. The demonstration was all that was keeping Daniel in London, and the moment it was done, she knew he would be leaving. The thought filled her with such despair that it almost blanked out the terror she felt at performing her experiment in front of what looked to be half of London. Almost. She swallowed a gulp of sickness as the president of the Royal Society introduced Ulysses to the cheering crowd.

The next hour passed quickly as she set up the apparatus while Daniel lectured. He spoke eloquently but simply, as she had advised, and had Penelope not known better, she would have sworn he truly had made the discoveries he was describing. Whenever she spared a glance at the audience she could see them listening with rapt attention, and the love she bore him grew ever more powerful. It would be impossible not to love a man who could hold hundreds in his sway, she thought, then resolutely turned her attention back to the matter at hand.

To finally prove the connection between electricity and magnetism, Penelope had fixed a magnet in a basin filled with mercury, and then dipped a wire connected to a Cruickshank battery into the middle of the mercury. When Daniel engaged the current, the upper end of the magnet moved in circles around the fixed wire, thus showing the relationship between the two forces. Penelope and Daniel performed the experiment twice, to prove the reaction had not been a fluke. When they finished, a heavy silence fell over the spectators. A second later they were on their feet, cheering with approval.

Penelope stood beside Daniel, tears in her eyes as emotion overwhelmed her. She felt pride and triumph at realizing her life's dream, to be sure, but she also felt a secret sense of resentment that the world would never know this was her accomplishment, not Ulysses's. The realization she should be so small-minded and selfish horrified her, but she could not deny the moment was bittersweet. She turned to Daniel to find him watching her, and the expression of pride and understanding in his eyes made her heart swell with love.

"You've done it," he said, his voice for her ears alone.

She blinked back tears. "I know."

"Yes, and I think it is time they knew it as well."

His cryptic answer puzzled her, but before she could demand an explanation he was stepping forward, holding up his hands to quiet the audience.

"I am a fraud," he announced, his voice ringing calm and cool through the lecture hall. "The person to whom you owe your cheers is not me, but my sister, Miss Penelope Grantham."

A shocked gasp filled the auditorium, and a few cries of disbelief rose from many of the scientists. Once more Daniel held up his hand, commanding silence. "It is true," he said, his green gaze sweeping over the audience. "This entire experiment was all her doing, and the apparatus you see behind me was built by her design, not mine. She is the genius, not I, and had it not been for her I should still be floundering about unable to prove my theories. I wish that she be given full recognition for her contributions, for all that she has done. Without her, this experiment would never have taken place."

If the audience was stunned by his revelation, Penelope was no less so. She could hardly credit he could be so daring. Then once more the audience was on its feet cheering, and this time she knew the cheers were for her.

"Penelope." Daniel was smiling, his hand held out for her. "What are you waiting for? Come accept your due."

She gazed at him, tears streaming down her cheeks. "I love you," she said, but over the roar of the crowd she wasn't certain if he could hear her heartfelt words.

"Well, thank heaven that is behind us." Penelope's mother sighed, indulging in an unladylike gulp of the French champagne Daniel had ordered brought up from the cellars. "You have carried it off, dearest boy, and managed to see this daughter of mine receive the credit she deserves in the process. I shall be forever in your debt."

"It was my pleasure, ma'am," he responded, graciously raising his glass first to her and then to Penelope. "Although I was doing no more than telling the truth."

His words brought yet another bout of tears to Penelope's eyes as she remembered standing on the podium, receiving the recognition she thought would never be hers. It had been the culmination of all her years of work, and even as she was curtseying to the cheering crowds, she could feel her heart breaking. She had realized her dreams, yes, but the cost was the man she loved.

She'd spent the past two nights telling herself that when the time came to say her goodbyes to Daniel, she would behave with dignity and courage. She wouldn't shed any more tears than one friend might reasonably expect at being parted from another, and she would on no account even allude to the love burning in her heart. But now that the moment was almost at hand, she knew she could not do it. She set her glass down and leapt to her feet.

"I . . . if you will excuse me, I believe I shall go up to my room," she said, when both her mother and Daniel turned to gape at her. "Speaking of my experiments just made me think of something, and I must write it down." She turned and fled before disgracing herself.

She had just reached the bottom of the steps when she felt Daniel grab her arm. "Penelope, what on earth is ailing you?" he demanded, whirling her around. At the sight of the tears on her cheeks, he gave an astonished gasp. "You're crying," he said, stating what to Penelope was patently obvious. "Is something wrong?"

"No, nothing's wrong!" she said desperately, trying frantically to free herself from his grip. "Now let me go, you oaf, so I can go upstairs." She tugged again when he wouldn't release her. "I said let me go, curse you!"

He stared down at her, his stunned look dissolving into a dazzling smile. "I don't believe so," he said slowly, his smile turning his eyes to purest emerald. "I don't believe so at all." Then he picked her up and carried her back into the parlor.

"Put me down!" she cried, embarrassed and enraged all at once. "Daniel Warfield, put me down this instant or I shall box your ears until you howl!"

"In a moment." Daniel controlled her struggles with an ease that was positively insulting. He turned to her mother, who was sitting on the settee with a look of comic confusion on her face.

"Mama, I should be obliged if you would kindly leave the room so I might propose to your daughter in private," he said, his arms tight about Penelope.

"Propose?" Penelope was stunned and then furious. He was making sport of her, she decided, tears streaming down her face as he set her on her feet. "Don't you dare leave!" she told her mother in an angry voice. "I'd as lief marry the devil as this villain!"

But her mama was already leaving, her glass of champagne forgotten as she clasped first Penelope and then Daniel to her bosom. "Oh, my dears, you have made me the happiest of women!" she sobbed, laughing and crying at the same time. "I knew you were right for one another. I knew it!"

Penelope listened in stunned disbelief, wondering if she had swooned and was imagining all of this. It couldn't be she thought dazedly, knowing if this was indeed all a dream, the disappointment would kill her.

"Now I shall be your mama in fact as well as fancy." Her mother was kissing Daniel's cheek. "I cannot tell you how proud I shall be to call you son."

"And I shall be delighted to call you mama," Daniel returned, pressing a kiss on Mrs. Grantham's cheek. "I adore you, but I am sure you will understand if I ask you to leave. I wish to be private with Penelope."

"Mama, don't you dare—"

"Say no more, my son," Penelope's mother said, ignoring her outburst. "I shall be gone in a thrice." She picked up her glass, a smile of maternal delight on her face as she bustled from the room.

The door closed behind her, and Penelope whirled around, fully prepared to do battle, only to find Daniel regarding her with that same dazed look on his face. An emotion she refused to recognize as hope flickered in her heart, and she ruthlessly tried to smother it.

"What are you gaping at?" she demanded, dashing her tears from her face with a shaking hand. "You look as foolish as a moonling standing there."

"Mayhap I feel like a moonling," he said, not seeming to take the slightest offense at her insulting words. "I haven't had complete use of my faculties since the moment you confronted me in the graveyard and asked if I wanted to impersonate your brother. That is the only explanation I can think of for what I am about to do."

Hope was almost as terrifying as love, Penelope discovered, taking a stumbling step back. "Wh-what are you about to do?" she asked, her heart beating so loud she thought he must surely hear it.

He followed her inexorably. "I am about to tell you I love you," he said softly, capturing her hand and pulling her into his arms. "I am about to ask you to be my wife." Then he bent his head and took her lips in a kiss of passion and demand.

At first Penelope was too shocked to resist, and then she was too happy, surrendering to the kiss with all the love she had kept bottled up deep inside her. This was everything she had ever wanted; *he* was everything she had ever wanted; and she gave him her heart and her soul without reservation or remorse.

"I love you, Penelope," he whispered, his voice shaking with urgency as he pressed kiss after kiss against her trembling mouth. "Tell me that you love me; let me hear the words."

"I love you," she said, going on tiptoe to press her own kisses against his mouth. "Oh, Daniel, I love you so very much. I was dying to think you were leaving, and I should never see you again!"

"Never!" he promised fervently, kissing and caressing her until they were both trembling with passion. Finally he drew back, his whole body shaking with the desire she had stirred in him.

"We must stop, my love, before your mama has cause to put a bullet through me," he said, taking her hand and guiding her to the settee. "But first things first. When will you marry me?"

"As soon as it can be arranged," she replied, dazed at the prospect of being his wife.

"I will be returning to America," he warned, eyeing her worriedly. "And I have decided not to challenge Andrew's right to the title. The world thinks Daniel Warfield is dead, and that is the way I prefer it."

"That is the way I prefer it as well," she said, sniffing back happy tears and feeling deliriously happy. She loved Daniel so much she didn't give a whit where they lived, so long as they were together. Only one thing troubled her, and she gave him a worried look as she spoke.

"What about me?" she asked, meeting his gaze levelly. "I am still a scientist, you know. A bluestocking, a—a learned lady who cares more for scientific experiments than the usual feminine arts. My needlework is abysmal, and Mama will tell you I know next to nothing about running a household. I—I would not have you marry me and then regret it."

This won her several gratifying kisses and an audacious caress that had her gasping in delight. "The only thing I could ever regret is not having you as my wife," he told her patiently. "You are the most wonderful woman in the world: difficult, obstreperous, as sharp tongued as a harpy, and I would not change a single thing about you. Now, will you marry me, or must I carry you off to America, and to the devil with convention?"

Penelope threw her arms about his neck and gave him a kiss of her own. "I have already said I would, you cloth head!" she scolded, laughing at his dazed response. "Now hurry and kiss me some more before Mama returns!"

Daniel was more than happy to oblige, and they were enjoying another passionate bout when a metallic rattling announced Mrs. Grantham's return. At least, that was what Daniel thought it was. He almost tumbled off the settee in shock when she entered accompanied by a rattling suit of armor that appeared to be occupied.

The contraption clanked and clattered as it advanced toward him, the hinges squeaking when the arms moved to lift the visor. A pair of faded hazel eyes regarded him quizzically, and the voice coming from deep within the suit seemed to squeak as well.

"So you are the varlet who has usurped my name, and is now making free with my sister's person," the creature accused in lofty accents. "Name your choice of weapons, sir, that I might meet you in mortal combat on the field of honor and restore my family's honor."

"Oh, do be quiet, Ulysses." Penelope spoke before Daniel

could find his voice. "Daniel has just asked me to marry him, and we want to be alone so that we can kiss. Mama, take him away."

"He asked you to marry him?" Ulysses's voice lost its medieval flavoring and he beamed first at Penelope and then at Daniel. "I say, that is capital! Welcome to the family, sir!"

"Thank you, I think," Daniel said, eyeing him wryly. "Will you need some help getting out of that thing?"

"Well, now that you mention it, I am rather stuck." There was a cacophony of squeaks and squawks as Ulysses waved his arms. "Do you think one of your servants might be willing to assist me? Mama and Penelope are never any use."

Daniel bit his lip, but managed to keep his composure. "I am sure they would be delighted. Now, please go."

Ulysses gave a much put-upon sigh. "Oh, very well." He lowered the visor with a clank. "Come, Mama," he said, and turned and rattled his way out of the room.

"Are you quite sure you still wish to marry me?" Penelope asked once they were alone. "Now that you've met Ulysses, I shouldn't blame you at all if you wanted to cry off."

He gave her a kiss to set her mind at ease. "I should marry you, my darling, if you had a dozen Ulysses clattering about the house. Hush now, and pay close attention; there is something I wish to teach you."

"Oh?" Her hand stole up to caress his cheek. "And pray, what might that be?"

"How to make love to your husband," he answered, gathering her close. "And I must warn you, I believe in teaching a very thorough lesson."

"Good." She reached up and kissed him a second time. "I have a feeling I may be in need of a great deal of instruction." And she kissed him with an expertise that belied that statement, but promised delight for many lessons to come.